REDWOOD CAFE

REDWOOD GROVE

CHRISTINE GAEL
SHAYLA CHERRY

Ava

HELLO! *You've reached the answering machine of Margaret Hoffman of Hoffman Farms. If this is a business call, you've got the wrong line. I'm retired, and you can go bother Nolan. If you know me as Gran, go ahead and leave a message. But if this is Echo Murray, don't even think of leaving me another eight-minute message about your latest dream. It took up so much room on my machine that the next message – from my great-granddaughter all the way up in Portland, mind – got cut off after ten seconds. You're welcome to tell me in person, like a reasonable human being.*

Ava winced at Nolan's name, but she let the recording play through to the end. Usually Gran answered midway through, but not today. Not this *week*, come to think of it. Had her decades-old rotary phone finally given up the ghost?

Ava hung up without leaving a message. She'd left three in as many days.

It wasn't like Gran to take so long to get back to her... though it wasn't the first time that had happened. The last time Ava got her grandmother on the phone, Gran had talked a mile a minute about her spring garden and the hundreds of varieties of seeds she had ordered months before. She was probably out in the garden now, kneeling over her rows of freshly turned soil and tucking seeds into the ground.

The image triggered a sharp, surprising pain in Ava's chest. Was she homesick for the place she had left twenty-five years ago? Maybe. More likely, she just missed her grandmother. They lived in the same state, but driving from San Diego to Gran's farm in northern California took at least nine hours – not exactly a weekend trip – and Ava didn't make it up as often as she would like... especially now that Nolan managed the farm. She had never made a decision to avoid him – had decided just the opposite, in fact, and told herself that she would never let his presence on the farm keep her away from Gran. But the truth of the matter was that, ever since Gran had hired Ava's high school sweetheart a few years back, Ava's trips to Hoffman Farm had been few and far between.

Whatever the reason, Ava suddenly felt claustrophobic in the tiny living room of her San Diego bungalow.

She should take a page out of Gran's book and get outside. The late spring morning offered a clear blue sky, with none of the fog that clouded so many mornings later in the year. Ava had plenty of time before her shift started, so she slipped on her walking shoes and trotted over to her neighbor's house to rap on her door. Isela answered right away, still wearing the flowered silk robe that she donned every day for her morning routine of coffee and a romance novel.

"I'm going to walk to work today," Ava said. "If you want to come with me, I'll give you a short stack on the house."

"Are they still making those matcha pancakes?" Isela asked.

Ava grinned. "Yup."

"Sold. Give me two minutes to change."

Ava turned her face to the sky as she waited for her friend, letting the sunshine warm her cheeks. She was a sun worshiper through and through. Every one of her forty-three years showed on her face, but Ava didn't mind. Like the tiger stripes that remained after her children were born, she had earned them, each and every one. And the sun wasn't unkind; the golden highlights in her hair and healthy color in her face more than made up for the fine lines on her forehead. Her grandmother's face was covered in wrinkles, and to Ava, she was still the most beautiful woman in the world. Gran had aged gracefully, and so would she.

When Isela was ready, they made their way south through their Pacific Beach neighborhood and crossed the busy main streets so that they could walk along the edge of Mission Bay. The rowers were out already, moving in perfect unison within the narrow confines of their needle-shaped boats, and Isela bumped her hip against Ava's.

"I wish you'd reconsider ZLAC." Isela had been talking up her new rowing club for weeks, trying to convince Ava to join her for practice on Saturday mornings at dawn.

"These old bones aren't seaworthy," Ava said in her best old-lady voice.

"You're two years younger than me, you faker!" Isela cackled. "You're a spring chicken, and you know it."

"Yes, but I've been a mother for twenty-four years to your eighteen. So in *mother* years..."

"Half of the women are in their sixties," her friend interrupted, "and they're stronger than the two of us put together."

Ava watched another group of women walk toward the water, carrying the long boat up on their shoulders. The camaraderie of it pulled at her heart, but she dreaded the thought of falling out of sync with the others and whopping some poor woman upside the head with her oar.

"It's just not my thing."

"You won't know that until you try it. It's the oldest women's rowing club in the world!"

"Imagine my joy," Ava said, deadpan. The women put their boat in the water, and Ava walked on.

"It's a full-body workout. And everyone there is so kind. You'd love it."

"I doubt that." She had played softball in high school, and while she'd loved the practices and camaraderie, she had dreaded every game. Nervous anticipation followed by the disappointment of her teammates when they lost.

But Isela wouldn't be dissuaded so easily. "You don't have to compete. You and I could take out the little two-person boats, just get out on the water and get some exercise. Think about it."

Exercise and camaraderie *without* competition? That sounded like something she could get on board with.

"Maybe," Ava conceded and then laughed as Isela whooped in victory.

Lord knew she needed *something* new in her life – and *not* those dating apps that her daughter kept trying to sell her on.

"You know what?" Isela said as they passed the rowing club. "I inspired *myself*. I'm going to get out on the water. They have one-woman boats, you know. Club members can take them out anytime. It's as close as you're likely to come to flying."

"Flying backwards sounds terrifying."

Isela laughed and then shrugged. "You get used to it."

"What about your pancakes?" Ava called as Isela walked into the boathouse.

"Maybe tomorrow! I'll see you here on Saturday. Seven sharp!"

"Maybe next week!" Ava teased, even though she was half convinced. She wouldn't be surprised to wake up to the sound of Isela knocking at her door at six-thirty on Saturday morning.

Ava walked along the bay, soaking up the sunshine for as long as she could before heading back through town to Sakura. The family-owned restaurant served a little bit of everything, from mochi pancakes to sushi dinners, and Ava had been working there for over a decade now. Mostly she stayed for the ocean view. She might never be able to afford a house on the beach, but she could at least enjoy a view of the water during her working hours. And her commute, if she took the long way around.

"Good morning, sunshine!" a singsong voice called as Ava walked in.

Ava grinned. "Good morning, Joan."

Nearly seventy years old, Joan still greeted the start of each shift with impressive good humor.

"I'm due for a break," Joan said as Ava slipped her apron on. "I'm going for a quick walk. Will you see to table ten? They just sat down."

"Of course," Ava replied.

It was a slow shift, the weekday brunch crowd, which always gave Ava too much time to think. More and more it seemed like something cold and sharp had been growing beneath her habitual gratitude for the comfortable life she'd built after her divorce. It was a good life, definitely better than living in the prison of a loveless marriage, and yet... some days, it all seemed to fall flat.

Her daughter Maggie lived way up in Portland, and her son Ryan was about to fly the nest, bent on following in his father's footsteps. Ava might have expected as much when she married a Marine, but the breath went out of her every time she thought of it. She would miss him terribly, despite hardly seeing him now. Ava's ex-husband owned a gorgeous house overlooking the beach in La Jolla, an easy mile from Ryan's school and most of his friends. He had outgrown Ava's tiny two-bedroom place years ago, and he had been spending more and more time at his dad's ever since starting high school. She would adjust to her new normal like she always did.

She sucked in a steadying breath and pasted on a smile as one of their regulars walked in the front door.

"Good morning, Kelly! The usual?"

From that point on, there was no space for her own worries. The restaurant quickly filled to capacity. Maybe that was the reason she still loved working as a server after all these years. It took so little to brighten someone's day; she could usually manage it with nothing but a smile and a kind word. And if *that* didn't work, a breakfast cupcake usually did the trick.

When her shift was over, she went down to the beach and kicked off her shoes for a walk in the sand. It was only after she spent a good twenty minutes unwinding from her day that she turned her cell phone back on.

Three missed calls from Toni.

She stopped where she stood, suddenly anchored in place by the scant layer of sand that covered her toes.

Something was wrong.

Panic clawed at her lungs as she stared at the picture she had assigned to Toni's number. Like most pictures of her bestie, it was dominated by a mass of glossy brown curls and a smile that lit up her whole face. Those curls were decked out with silver streaks these days. Aside from that minor adornment, Toni hadn't changed much over the years. While they still talked on the phone a couple times a week, it was completely unlike Toni to call her multiple times in a day, let alone three times in a row.

Ava gathered her courage and called her friend back.

Whatever it was, they could handle it together.

"Ava!" Toni sounded out of breath. "Oh, thank goodness. Hi."

"What's wrong?" Ava demanded.

Toni only took a beat before replying, but it felt like an eternity.

"Gran's in the hospital."

Ava shook her head, sinking down into the sand as dread

rolled through her. Her grandmother hated hospitals. Like, 'I'll go in a body bag and not a minute sooner' hated them. For a split second, some irrational corner of her mind tried to tell her that Toni was talking about someone else. But no. The only person that Toni had ever called Gran was Ava's grandmother. At five years old, she had been convinced that Gran was the woman's name.

"Ava? Are you there?"

"Yeah." Ava nodded and swallowed. "Go on."

"She collapsed at the grocery store, and they took her to a hospital in San Jose. That's all I know."

"Who told you?"

"Echo called me."

"You're sure she wasn't relaying a premonition?" Ava joked weakly.

"She was there when it happened, and she didn't have your number."

Ava squeezed her eyes shut. "Okay. If I leave now, I can be there by tonight."

"Don't break any traffic laws getting here. I can be there in an hour. She won't be alone. Drive safe, okay?"

"Okay."

"And Ava?"

"Yeah?" She waited for her friend to say that it was all a mistake, Gran was home, she was fine.

"I love you."

Ava swallowed. "I love you too, Toni. See you soon."

2

Beth

GOLDEN LIGHT CREPT through the trees as Beth Merrill hiked through the woods, feeling like a bona fide grownup. It was her first full day in California and, despite her boyfriend's refusal to get out of bed before ten, she was determined to enjoy every minute of it.

Fat yellow banana slugs longer than her boots made their way across the forest floor. She was the only one on the trail this early in the morning, and it felt like she had the whole mountainside to herself.

There was a sudden motion up ahead, and Beth froze. A bobcat paused in the middle of the trail and regarded her with calm golden eyes. Time seemed to stop as they looked at each other, and Beth's breath caught in her chest. The wildcat was gorgeous, with a thick tawny-colored coat covered in black markings. The fur on its chest was lighter, almost white, with broad black stripes running across the fur on its legs. It was bigger than a fox, with a regal scruff under its cheeks and black tufts of fur coming up from the tips of its ears.

It was probably less than five seconds before the bobcat turned and disappeared back into the grass, but Beth's whole body was buzzing from that encounter for the rest of her hike. She sailed through miles of field and forest with all of the energy in the world, elated by her encounter with one of the most beautiful animals she had ever seen. She couldn't wait to tell her family back in Maine. Especially her Aunt Anna, who was an amazing wildlife photographer. She'd have loved to see it.

Beth shoved back a wave of homesickness and headed back to her car. By the time she got there, she was starving. Coffee and granola bars had gotten her through the first half of her morning, but she was ready for a real breakfast. She turned her car into town, hoping that Redwood Grove would have at least one little café open on a weekday morning. If she had to drive all the way back to Half Moon Bay before she got some food, she might starve.

Beth was in luck. There *was* a restaurant open: a charming two-story building across the street from the grocery store. A huge wooden sign hanging out front said *Redwood House.*

She skipped up the front steps of the old building and peeked inside. The interior was modern, with well-spaced wooden tables and The Lumineers crooning over the speakers. Once Beth caught someone's attention, she chose a sunny table on the broad front porch.

She was still waiting on her eggs Benedict when a little woman with vast clouds of white hair paused at the top of the stairs and stared at her. Beth glanced uncertainly over her shoulder, but there was no one else on the porch, so she looked back at the old lady and smiled. "Hello."

"You have the loveliest aura," the woman murmured, drifting closer. She had a gauzy look about her that might have been almost spectral had the colors not been so bright. Printed silks in varied jewel tones draped her from her shoulders to her feet, and even her cloud of snowy white hair was braided with bright bits of color. "Pale gold, like a sunrise. It's rare to see such a pure, untainted aura these days. It's quite lovely."

"Thank you?" Beth couldn't quite keep her tone from tilting up into a question at the end, but the smile that she gave the old lady was genuine. Eccentric as she was, there was something about her that made her impossible to dislike. She seemed entirely genuine. "My name is Beth."

"I'm Echo," the old lady said with a brilliant smile. She had the sort of wrinkles that softened her face into something beautiful, and there was an energetic glow to her bright brown eyes. She paused for a moment, then gestured to the chair across from Beth. "May I?"

"Sure," Beth said readily. She had never liked eating alone.

"It's your first time in Redwood Grove," Echo said. It wasn't a question.

"It is," Beth said. "You live here?"

Echo grinned and nodded. "What brings you to our little town, Beth?"

"I was just exploring the skyline trail," Beth said, "and I stopped in for something to eat."

"Fate," Echo said with a sage nod.

Beth blinked at her, not sure what to say to that. So she smiled and shared the most exciting part of her morning. "I saw a bobcat on the trail. It was so beautiful."

"A bobcat!" Echo exclaimed, rocking backwards in shock. Then she nodded. "Lynx rufus. Yes. Of course."

The waitress dropped Beth's food at the table, and Beth greeted her with a word of thanks.

"Your usual?" the server asked Echo. The old lady nodded, still staring at Beth.

"You know what the lynx symbolizes, don't you?" she asked as the waitress walked away.

Beth's mouth was full of bread and hollandaise. She shook her head.

"You need time by yourself to reflect," Echo said solemnly. "Time to discover your own inner strength. The lynx sees truth in the heart of others, and she needs no one's approval but her own. She appeared to warn you to keep your distance from those who do not truly care for you. You will soon see through the masks worn by those in your life who do not show you their true face."

Beth swallowed her food and stared at Echo. What could she say to that?

Even as one part of her mind dismissed the woman's words, they went straight to Beth's heart. Nearly all of her friends from college had fallen off the map since graduation last year.

Echo smiled gently and patted Beth's hand. "The bobcat symbolizes patience and solitude. She may appear to those who are afraid of being alone. The time has come to discover who you truly are, apart from anyone else and their expectations."

Echo pulled something out from the many layers of fabric that she wore. It was a woven bit of twine, similar to the friendship bracelets that Beth had made as a little girl. But this was made with some sort of natural material in tones of sage green and earthy gold. Beth put out her hand and allowed Echo to tie it around her wrist.

"There," Echo said with satisfaction. She gave Beth a bright smile and stood. "A reminder. Let it steady you through the difficult times to come."

Beth ran her fingertips over the bracelet, feeling the intricate pattern. "Thank you."

"You are never truly alone, Beth." Echo put a hand on Beth's curls in benediction. "You're stronger than you know. I'll see you again soon."

"I, um, thank you," Beth said as Echo walked inside. "See you... later."

Beth scarfed down the rest of her breakfast, hardly tasting it. She wasn't sure what to make of Echo's nebulous predictions. They seemed foreboding, and yet Beth simply felt... fortified. Ready to leave her college years behind and face whatever came next. She wandered down Redwood Grove's charming main street—as far as she could tell, its *only* commercial street—in the hope of finding some pastries to bring home.

And that's when she saw the yarn shop.

And the help wanted sign in the window.

Beth had an immediate feeling of kismet. She had intended to start her job search tomorrow when Josh went off to work. Her plan had been to cast a wide net; she wasn't picky. Baking, waitressing, childcare... Beth was good at plenty of odd jobs. Finding work to pay the bills while she figured out what was next would have been easy enough, and she had planned to look for something near their new apartment in Half Moon Bay.

But knitting. Knitting was what she *loved*. She loved the excitement of a fresh skein of yarn and the challenge of a new pattern. When her nerves were raw, the meditative repetition of the work soothed her. And there was nothing like the satisfaction of wearing something that she had designed and knitted herself, or seeing the look on a loved one's face when she presented them with a fresh gift. Being *paid* to talk about yarn all day would be a dream come true. And Redwood Grove wasn't too terribly far from Half Moon Bay. The short ride was a ridiculously gorgeous stretch of coastal highway followed by a winding mountain road...

Beth just about sprinted up the steps.

Imagine Knit was housed in a gorgeous old Victorian building; the ornate woodwork out front was painted in rich hues of crimson and teal. The front door was a shocking shade of red, and of course the interior of the store was absolutely bursting with color. Before she had even closed the door behind her, Beth felt at home.

The walls were stocked from floor to ceiling with every sort of yarn. Pastel cotton and jewel-toned merino, undyed alpaca and chunky cashmere... just *looking* at them fed Beth's soul. She could have spent the next two hours just stroking the skeins of yarn and dreaming up what she wanted to make with each one... but instead, she honed in on the iron-haired lady behind the counter and walked right up to her.

"Good morning. My name is Beth Merrill."

"Yolanda," the woman returned with a tired smile. "Can I help you find something, Beth?"

"I'm here about the job. I don't have my resume with me – I was just passing through and I saw the sign in the window – but I could fill out a form if you have one or come back with–"

"Do you knit, Beth?" Yolanda interrupted. "Do you know how to crochet?" Her eyes were a deep shade of brown, and she spoke with the faint accent of someone who had adopted English as her second language long before Beth was even born.

"I love to knit," Beth assured her. "I know how to crochet, but it's not really my thing. Knitting, though... I'm really good, Miss Yolanda. I could answer just about any question your customers would have. I even have some of my original colorwork patterns available on Ravelry."

"When can you start?"

Beth stared at her for a second before realizing that her mouth was hanging open, and she snapped it shut. "I... I can start anytime you like. You... Don't you want references, or...?"

Yolanda waved a hand in dismissal. "Strangers' opinions carry no weight with me, *mijita*. And I'm too old to be working the floor every day. The last girl left with no notice, and I'm tired. We'll try you out and see how you do. So. When can you start?"

"Tomorrow?" Beth asked, shaky with excitement. She half wanted to say *Right now!* But Josh would start to worry, and her phone had died after one too many pictures of wildflowers and banana slugs.

"Eight o'clock?" Yolanda asked.

"I'll be here. Thank you so much for the opportunity. You won't be disappointed."

"We'll see," the iron-haired old lady replied. But her eyes brightened a bit, and she favored Beth with a grin. "Here." She reached under the counter and put several tiny balls of scrap yarn in a bag. "Bring me some original colorwork so I know what you can do."

"Thank you," Beth said again. "I will."

The morning clouds had melted away by the time Beth drove back down through the mountains to Highway One, and the sun shone off of the ocean with glorious brilliance as she drove up the coast. Beth couldn't remember the last time she had felt this happy. Everything was going her way. She couldn't wait to tell Josh about her new job, not to mention her encounters with a California bobcat and a local eccentric.

But when she walked into their new apartment, it was like walking into a thick fog. Josh sat on the couch with his head down, and Beth could feel misery radiating from him in waves.

"Josh?" she said hesitantly. "What's wrong?"

"I messed up, Beth." He looked up at her, his face twisted with remorse.

She shook her head, uncomprehending. "What do you mean?"

"I don't want to do this anymore."

"Th-this," Beth stuttered and sucked in a breath. "You mean California? The new job?"

"Not the job," Josh said miserably. "I'm sorry. I should have told you weeks ago. I never should have let you follow me out here. I thought– but it's not working. I'm not happy anymore."

The paper bag of scrap yarn fell from Beth's hand, and she leaned against the wall to steady herself. "What are you saying?"

"I don't think we should be together. I want to break up."

3

Ava

"VISITING HOURS ENDED AT EIGHT," said the woman ensconced in the fortress-like nurses' station.

"That's what they told me downstairs," Ava said. "But I need to–"

The woman didn't look away from her computer screen, but she held a hand up toward Ava's face to stem her explanation. "You can come back at eleven o'clock tomorrow."

"I drove here from San Diego," Ava pleaded, trying to steady her voice. A long, stressful drive and gas-station coffee had left her nerves jumpier than a rabbit in bobcat country. "I just found out about my grandmother today. Please, there must be someone I can talk to."

The woman gave her a flat, unfriendly look as she stood and gathered a stack of folders to her chest. "Eleven o'clock tomorrow. If you need a place to stay, there's a motel just down the street." She turned and walked away.

Ava stared after the woman in misleadingly cheerful pink scrubs, feeling like the air had gone out of her chest. Would she have to go door to door, peeking into strangers' rooms? Would she be able to find Gran before hospital security kicked her out? She couldn't just leave... but she couldn't do anything that would get her barred from the hospital, either.

"What's your grandmother's name?"

Ava jumped in surprise and turned to find the source of the question. Another nurse walked down the hall, into the bright fluorescent lights above the floor's main desk. This woman's face was friendly, and Ava felt a fragile spark of hope kindle in her chest.

"Margaret Hoffman."

"Oh, you must be Nolan's sister," the woman said brightly. "I'm Priya. Nice to meet you."

Nolan. The name hit Ava like a kick to the gut, and she had to click her teeth shut after her jaw dropped. But before Ava could correct her, Priya turned and set off down the hallway. Ava followed her as the other woman continued on.

"Your cousin Toni was here earlier – she brought the most gorgeous bouquet of flowers – but she got booted out at eight. Nolan was in this morning with chicken broth. Marge got a good bit of it down before she fell asleep. That's always such a good sign. She's a fighter, that one," Priya continued as they rounded a corner. "They can get a little strict about visitation because our patients need rest above all, but in my opinion, what they really need is to rest surrounded by family. It's so nice to see you all show up for your grandmother. I'll tell you, it just about breaks my heart when we have old folks in here without a single visitor. They can't heal in isolation, not really."

Ava's stomach sank with guilt as she thought of the time her grandmother had already spent in the hospital without her.

"She's been in and out," Priya whispered as she opened the door. The room was dimly lit, and she entered on tiptoe. "Still sleeping."

Ava saw the flowers first, straight across from the door. Bright orange calendula, dainty white feverfew, brilliant blue cornflower... all of Gran's favorite medicinal flowers. Her eyes passed over an array of blinking lights and went straight to her grandmother.

The sight of her cut Ava's heart in two.

Gran looked terrible. Emaciated and pale, with a tent of blankets over her feet. What had happened to her hale, lively grandmother? This wasn't the Margaret Hoffman she knew. How had she changed so drastically so quickly? Ava had just seen her a few months ago, and Gran had sounded like her normal self a few *days* ago on the phone.

Shock had moved her from the door to Gran's bedside without any awareness of her footsteps. Priya was still talking, but her words didn't register. Gran's hand was cold in hers, so icy that Ava felt a jolt of fear. But she could see her grandmother's chest moving up and down under the blankets, and the monitor beside the bed showed a comforting pattern of hills and valleys. She turned to ask Priya for another blanket or a hot water bottle, but the nurse was gone.

Ava stood stranded at the bedside, holding her grandmother's hand in her own. She was too exhausted to think, too full of frantic energy to sit down. Her mind was a haze of guilt and fear that left little room for coherent thought. Eventually, when the storm of emotion had abated a bit, Ava released her grandmother's hand. She found a hot water bottle in a cabinet and filled it with warm water from the sink, then tucked it into bed with Gran.

The door opened behind her, and Ava turned, hoping to speak to a doctor and find out why Gran was here in the first place.

Instead, she locked eyes with Nolan Pasternak.

Ava froze.

Seeing him again, here, now, was more than her brain could process. He looked so different from the boy she had seen every day of their high school years... and yet exactly the same. Teal green eyes, thick brown hair, that long nose. Still Nolan.

"Ava," he said, looking as shell-shocked as she felt. "Hi."

"Why did no one call me?" Ava asked. She winced at her own voice, hating the tone of accusation and anger. But dang it, she *was* angry.

Nolan's mouth worked soundlessly for a few seconds before he said, "Toni called you, didn't she?"

"I mean when Gran collapsed." She had to force herself to keep her voice down.

Nolan looked down at the thermos he held with two hands. "I didn't have your number, and I didn't feel comfortable going through her things to find it... or your mother's," he added with a questioning glance.

God, her mother. Ava looked away, focusing on her grandmother. She supposed she should call Lyra at some point and let her know what was going on. That was a problem for tomorrow. Ava took Gran's hand in hers, trying to warm her icy fingers.

"I'm sorry," Nolan said from behind her. "I should have gotten in touch with you somehow. But between running the farm and trying to advocate for Gran…"

Gran's fingers tightened on hers, and Ava leaned closer. "Gran? It's me. I'm here."

"Lyra?" Gran looked at Ava, her eyes half focused. Her grip was strong, but her voice held a fear that Ava had never heard before. "Don't let them take my leg, Lyra. Get me out of here."

"It's okay," Ava said, blinking back tears. "It's okay, I'm here."

"Where's the baby?" Gran asked, already drifting back to sleep. "Who's taking care of Ava?"

Ava swallowed a sob that rose in her throat and looked helplessly at Nolan.

"It's the meds," he assured her. There was such a depth of compassion in his eyes that Ava felt a full second of free fall before she wrenched her gaze back to Gran. "She's as sharp as ever. Just on a lot of pain meds right now. It's been less than twenty-four hours since her surgery."

Ava looked up sharply. "What surgery?"

Nolan looked over at Gran, maybe wondering whether or not she was fully asleep. Then he looked back to Ava and gestured to the plastic chairs that sat in a corner, past the flowers.

"Sit down for a minute, would you? How about a cup of broth? You might as well drink it while it's warm. I'll bring more for Gran tomorrow."

Ava nodded, only half listening. There was a note on the

table, one corner stuck under the vase for safekeeping. She walked over and picked it up.

Ava,

I'm sorry I couldn't stay. Lizzie needed me to watch her girls. Gran was awake for a little while, and I told her you were on your way. She'll get through this, Ava. We'll get through this together. I'll be back in the morning with breakfast and some tea for Gran, okay?

Love,

Toni

Ava tucked the note in her pocket and sat down in one of the plastic chairs. Nolan poured a cup of broth and handed it to her; it was warm in her hands, perfect to drink. She took a long sip and immediately felt a bit steadier. It was a rich, nourishing broth, chicken and veggies and a healthy squeeze of lemon. Nolan pulled the other chair so that it was sitting at an angle, half facing Ava and half facing Gran's hospital bed.

"What's wrong with her?" Ava's voice was still shaky, despite the broth. "Did they tell you?"

"Apparently she had an infection in her leg that wouldn't heal. It had been sapping her strength, and then it got bad fast. They did what they could, but... they had to amputate."

Ava startled so badly that broth sloshed over the edge of her cup. "*Her leg?*" She wanted to scream, but she managed to keep her voice to a horse whisper. "They took her *leg?*"

"Below the knee," Nolan confirmed solemnly. "It was her leg or her life."

"Who- she-" Ava stuttered and stopped. She set the broth aside and found a paper towel dispenser by the sink to dry her hands. This bit of news had rattled her so badly that she wanted to fall to her knees and sob, but Ava refused to let her tears fall. She could cry tears of relief – or, God forbid, tears of grief – when this was all over. Right now, Gran needed her to be strong.

When she had recovered enough to string a sentence together, Ava turned to Nolan and said, "She never would have agreed to that."

"She consented. They couldn't have done it otherwise. She signed the forms. She just has too much morphine in her system to remember right now."

Ava shook her head and leaned back against the counter, staring across the room at the tenting above Gran's feet.

Gran's *foot*.

Her knees felt like they might give out on her. Gran in a wheelchair? She wouldn't even be able to get into her house. Or into her *garden*... Her fiercely independent, active grandmother... how would she survive this?

"Why didn't she tell me?" Ava whimpered. Belatedly, she realized that her face was streaked with tears and snot. She turned away and grabbed another paper towel. After blowing her nose, she looked at Nolan and asked, "Why didn't anyone tell me she was sick?"

"She didn't tell anyone." Nolan's shoulders were hunched, and Ava could sense the same guilt radiating off of him that she felt deep in her gut. "You know how she is. Tried to take care of it herself until it was too late and she just collapsed in the grocery store."

Ava just shook her head. She was overtaken by a sudden memory, childhood-bright against the gray gloom of the hospital.

She could see her grandmother, not much older than Ava was now, standing in the spring sunshine. Gran had tilled up a whole garden patch just for Ava and another for Toni. She could still feel the excitement of poring over seed catalogs with Gran on cold winter days, the sense of importance that she had felt as she tucked each of her carefully chosen seeds into the rich soil of Gran's back garden that spring.

I've got every sort of medicine I'll ever need right here, Gran always said as she tended to her herb garden. Ava had always been more interested in tomatoes and carrots, in the treasure hunt of digging up potatoes... and of course in the acres and acres of strawberries that kept her fed and clothed as a child. But she could still see Toni at five and six and seven, listening with wide-eyed focus as Gran extolled the medicinal properties of her herbs and flowers.

I'll tell you girls a secret. The plants give us everything we'll ever need. Gardens give us life. Hospitals are where people go to die. You'll never catch me inside of one. I was born on this land. I gave birth on this land. And when my time comes, I'll die on this land.

"Ava?"

She nearly jumped out of her skin when Nolan put his hand on her shoulder. "What?"

"You look exhausted. Do you want me to drive you back to the farm?"

Ava shook her head so quickly that the room spun. "I want to be here when she wakes up."

Nolan nodded and squeezed Ava's shoulder gently before letting go. "I should be getting back. I'll give you my number, in case you or Gran want anything from home." He jotted his number down on a pad of paper and left it on Gran's bedside table. Before he left, he moved one of the chairs to Gran's bedside so that Ava could sit beside her.

As he moved toward the door, Ava reached out and grabbed his hand. It was an impulsive act, the panicked grasp of a drowning woman. She wanted to ask him to stay. To charm the nurses if they came to kick her out. Instead, she said, "Thank you. For everything."

Nolan nodded and squeezed her hand. His palm was strong and smooth, with the broad calluses of a man who worked every day of his life.

So different from the hand she had held at fifteen.

"She means a lot to... all of us. If she asks, tell her I'm feeding the animals." He gave her a crooked smile that was like a flash of light through the gloom. "All of them."

When Nolan was gone, the room felt horribly grim. Ava spoke to Gran, feeling awkward at first, then less so. Gran seemed to be deep in sleep, and she probably wouldn't hear or remember a thing than Ava said... but it filled the silence. It let her know that she wasn't alone.

"You've always been there for me, Gran. You took Lyra in when my dad left and she couldn't pay the rent. You took care of me when *she* left, even when she stayed away for years at a time. You treated my best friend like she was your own family. You were the first person to hold Maggie after she was born."

Ava took a shuddering breath. She wanted to put her face in the hospital blankets and cry, but she wouldn't. She wouldn't worry her grandmother. It was *her* turn to take care of *Gran*, not the other way around.

"I haven't always been there for you the way I should have been. The way you've been there for me. I was so caught up with taking care of Maggie and Ryan. And then, even when they didn't need me anymore... it never even occurred to me that *you* might. I guess, to me... you always seemed invincible."

Ava paused and swiped at her nose. She wasn't sure how long the restaurant could spare her or how she would pay rent in the meantime, but that was a problem for tomorrow. She would stay until her grandmother was out of this hospital... one way or another. Ava scooted a bit closer to the bed so that she could lean against the edge of the mattress as she held her grandmother's hand.

"You go ahead and rest, Gran. I'm not going anywhere."

4

Toni

Toni's truck crawled along the freeway so slowly that she could have outpaced the cars on foot. She should have known better than to drive to San Jose at eight in the morning, but it just hadn't occurred to her how absurdly packed the freeway would be. Rush hour had never been a part of her reality, and neither had Silicon Valley. She'd grown up fairly close to San Francisco and San Jose, but Toni had never been able to spend more than a few hours in a city without feeling like she wanted to crawl out of her skin.

Despite rush hour traffic, she made it to the hospital before the official visiting hours. But she was in luck; the severe nurse from the night before had gone home, and the current shift made no move to stop her when she hurried past the nurses' station to Gran's room.

Toni's heart cracked at the sight of her heart's family in

that dim, gray little room. Gran was passed out, looking no better than she had the night before. Ava was asleep too, perched on a chair and draped over the hospital railing of Gran's bed. She must have been dead tired to fall asleep in that impossibly uncomfortable position. At the first little noise – the quiet thump of the thermos on the side table as Toni set down the soup she had brought – Ava sat up with a start. She stood and turned. As soon as she saw Toni, her eyes filled with tears.

"I know," Toni said, blinking back tears of her own as she pulled Ava into a hug. "I know."

Ava pulled back to look at her. Her eyes were pink from crying, which made the blue of her irises look even brighter than usual. Her cheeks, on the other hand, were missing their usual healthy color. "We've gotta get her out of here, Toni."

Toni pushed dirty blond hair out of her friend's face and tucked it behind her ears. "We will. Just as soon as she's strong enough. Has she woken up at all?"

Ava shrugged and glanced over at Gran. "For a little while this morning. When the nurses came to change her dressings. They made me wait in the hall. I could still hear her." She gave Toni a shaky smile. "Giving them hell. I came back in. After. She recognized me."

"Of course she recognized you!" Toni exclaimed.

Ava just shrugged, looking over at Gran. It killed her to see Ava so shaken up, speaking in choppy sentences. Dark circles hung under her eyes. She needed a good night's rest in a real bed... but Toni would settle for getting some food into her. She hefted the bag of food she carried onto the table.

"I brought you chicken salad and coleslaw. There are some scones from the bakeshop in there too, and a thermos full of chai. The big thermos there has nettle soup for Gran. It's her recipe, fish stock and all."

Ava smiled, but it was a shadow of her usual grin. "She'll like that. Thank you."

"Toni?" Gran's voice was surprisingly strong, and Toni grinned as she took two quick steps toward the hospital bed.

"Ready for some nettle soup, Gran?"

She smiled and patted Toni's hand, which she took as a yes. As Toni turned to pour out a small serving of the pureed soup, Ava pushed a button that brought the back of Gran's hospital bed up with a slow whir.

"Avalon," Gran said in a voice that was exhausted and elated all at once. "When did you get here?"

Ava looked stricken, and Toni answered for her. "Ava's been here all night, Gran."

"Oh." Gran frowned as she accepted the cup of nettle soup. "Yes. Of course."

"Why didn't you call me?" Ava asked in a broken voice. "I would have come sooner."

Gran looked down into her cup. "It all happened so fast, chickadee. I didn't think the cut on my leg was any big thing. It was slow to heal, but I just kept on with my salves and my teas... and then I had a dizzy spell at the store. And I woke up here, not even sure where *here* was, and there were doctors standing over me with forms telling me that it was my leg or my life. And, well, I wasn't quite ready to go yet. I'd sooner gimp around the farm than not see it again. Or you." She looked up at them with a shaky smile. "It's lovely to see you girls together."

Gran's voice was tight, and it wasn't until she shifted her body and winced that Toni realized how badly her leg was hurting her. That woman had a tolerance for pain that beggared belief – Toni had once seen her slice her thumb to the bone and barely flinch as she bandaged herself up – so she could only imagine what sort of pain Gran was in now. Her pain meds had just about worn off, Toni realized. That was why Gran was finally awake and coherent. She squeezed Ava's arm and slipped away to find a nurse.

Half a cup of nettle soup and her next dose of medication put Gran right back to sleep. Toni tried to coax Ava to come back with her, but Ava wouldn't hear of it.

"Gran's doctors haven't been by once. I can't leave until I talk to them. I'll track them down today if they don't come to see her, and I'll sleep at Gran's house tonight."

"Good plan," Toni told her. "I wish I could stay, but Lizzie's usual babysitter is still sick, and I have a million things I need to get done before I watch the girls again tonight." Hospital visits and time with her nieces had left Toni woefully unprepared for the Saturday farmers market, which brought in the bulk of her income. She would still be able to manage it, but only if she got in a few hours of work before going over to her sister's house that evening.

"I can't believe you came all this way just to bring us some food," Ava said, pulling her into a hug.

"It was good to hear Gran sounding more like herself," Toni said, squeezing her friend tightly. "I'm sorry that I can't come back tonight, but if Lizzie misses another shift–"

"It's okay," Ava said. "Maybe I'll stay another night."

"Ava, no. You need sleep."

"I'll sleep when I'm dead," Ava said with a smile that didn't quite reach her eyes. She was quoting Gran.

Toni sighed in defeat. "At least eat something. I'll be back tomorrow."

"Thank you, Toni."

She made a fist and gave Ava a gentle tap under her chin like Gran used to do. "Keep your chin up, buttercup."

As Toni pulled up the dirt drive to her house, her first sight of home eased her worried heart. Late spring was Toni's favorite time of year. The garden was verdant and lush and exploding with color. Her garden ran the gamut from scarlet snapdragons to ultraviolet butterfly bush. And the *smell* of her garden was like no place else on Earth. Toni breathed deeply as she stepped down from her truck. The heady smell of lavender mixed with the sharp musk of calendula and the aroma of sun-warmed basil. There was little that she couldn't grow in the forgiving climate of the central coast, especially in this little garden tucked into a low spot in the mountains.

Toni moved slowly on her way up to the house, savoring the day. Thousands of bees filled the air with their hum. They were particularly thick around the purple-blue stars of the borage plants that stood at the southern edge of her garden. The industrious ladies buzzing around the dainty flowers of her holy basil had bright red pollen baskets, setting them apart from the usual parade of yellow and gold.

She wouldn't cut bouquets until the morning of the farmers market. On market days, she ventured out into her garden well before dawn. But there were a million other things to do in the meantime. She would start with gathering calendula to run through her dehydrators. Her body oils and salves were ready for market, but she needed more dried herbs for tea.

The sun had started its afternoon descent toward the ocean by the time Toni finished gathering herbs. Just as she started to walk back to the house with her full baskets, an unfamiliar car came up the drive. Someone stepped out of the passenger side, and the car drove away. The young woman had short, spiky hair and an oversized jacket that hung down to her knees; it was a moment before Toni recognized her brother's daughter.

"Juniper!" Toni shouted. In a voice that Juniper was still too far away to hear, Toni added, "What have you done to your hair?"

Her oldest niece had several new piercings, Toni noticed as they hurried toward each other, and she had applied her eyeliner that morning with a heavy hand. Toni didn't keep up with the latest trends, but she was fairly certain that this wasn't it. Her niece's style reminded her more of porcupine quills than decorative plumage.

"Hi, Nia." Juniper was the only one who called her that. It was an early childhood attempt at her name that had stuck. She looked shy within her protective garb, as if unsure of her welcome.

"What are you doing here?" Toni asked as she pulled Juniper into a hug. "Why aren't you in school?"

Juniper pulled back from her aunt's embrace. The girl's eyes were glassy with tears as she looked out over Toni's garden, but she affected a bitter smile. "Mom relapsed again."

"Oh, Junebug," Toni murmured. "I am so, so sorry."

Juniper laughed in a harsh way that was heartbreaking to hear from a sweet girl of sixteen. "I don't know why I thought this time would be any different. We should know better by now."

Toni rubbed Juniper's arm through her thick canvas jacket. "That doesn't make it any easier."

Juniper finally met her aunt's gaze, and the tears in her eyes spilled over. "Why does she never stay?"

Tears filled Toni's own eyes, and she opened her arms to her niece. "I don't know, sweetheart."

Juniper hesitated for just a moment... and then she fell into Toni's arms and wept like the broken-hearted girl she was.

5

Beth

"I can be on the next flight out there."

"No, Mom. You can't leave the restaurant. And I don't need you to. It'll be fine."

"You are more important to me than anything, Beth," Nikki said. "Maritza can manage the kitchen for a few days."

Beth's mother sounded like she was on the verge of tears, and Beth half regretted calling her. Nikki had enough on her plate without feeling like she needed to fly to her daughter's rescue. Beth was a grown woman, wasn't she? She didn't need her mommy to come save her.

"I'll be okay, Mom," Beth said again. "This is something that I need to get through on my own. At least give me a couple days to figure out what I'm going to do."

"I don't want you driving cross country by yourself,"

Nikki worried. "We could drive together, or I could help you sell the car and we could fly home."

Beth collapsed onto her couch with a huff of frustration. "I don't even know where I'm going to live."

"Come home to Cherry Blossom Point. You can stay with me while you decide what's next. Mateo may have renovated the rest of the house, but my kitchen and your bedroom are untouched. They're just like you remember them."

Moving home to the lurid purple walls of the bedroom that she had decorated as a teenager was the absolute last thing that Beth wanted. She took a deep breath and sank into the collapsed cushions of a second-hand sofa that was probably older than she was.

"Josh is spending the rest of this week with some high school buddies in San Francisco, so I have time to decide what I want to do. There's a little old lady at the yarn store that I'd hate to disappoint. I have to go tell her that I won't be able to start work today after all. I want to be there when she opens, so I should get ready to go."

"Okay," Nikki said with obvious reluctance. "Oh, Beth. I wish I could give you a hug and make you a huge dish of Monster Mac'n'Cheese."

"Thanks, Mom," Beth said, blinking back tears as she thought of her favorite childhood dish. The spinach-green jalapeno cheese sauce was *still* her favorite. "Me too. I'll call you later today, okay?"

"Okay, sweetheart. I love you."

"I love you too."

Beth hung up and just sat there for a minute, staring at the peeling paint on the front door of her ex-boyfriend's apartment. Josh hadn't given her much of a reason for breaking up with her. He'd just talked about how he had been feeling more and more distant from her for some time now, and how he needed to figure out who he was outside of a relationship. He seemed to be wracked with guilt, knowing how truly terrible his timing was.

"You were so excited to go that I didn't know how to tell you I would rather go by myself," he'd admitted the day before. "I kept trying to convince myself that it would be fun, that we could make a fresh start of it out here... but I've been lying to myself the whole time. I just don't feel *that way* about you anymore. And I can't keep pretending that I do."

He had left then, and Beth had sobbed her heart out on the kitchen floor. It had been a couple of hours before she had finally gotten her breath back to call her mom. Nikki was already at the restaurant by then, and she had missed her call. So Beth had called her friend Kiera, the only person her age that she felt truly close to anymore.

"Forget him," Kiera had said with the easy dismissal of someone who had never been in love. "What do *you* want to do?"

"I don't know what I want," Beth had said brokenly. "I followed him all the way across the country, and he doesn't even want me around."

"Then he's an idiot, and you're better off without him. It's time to figure out what matters to *you*."

Beth went to the kitchen sink and washed her face with cold water. Keeping her word mattered to her. That was a start. She had promised to be at Imagine Knit first thing that morning, and Beth Merrill kept her promises. A pair of jeans and a handmade sweater - dark blue with intricate white snowflakes - had her feeling somewhat like herself again. She forced down a lemon poppyseed muffin and a cup of coffee to balance out her sleepless night. Then she walked down to the parking lot to find her car, a little red Honda that had proven to be far more reliable than her boyfriend.

Ex-boyfriend, Beth corrected herself as she climbed inside.

She'd hardly slept, and by sunrise, she'd felt more numb than heartbroken. Her spirits lifted just a bit as she drove south on Highway One. The sky was pure blue without a cloud in sight, and the horizon was as far away as she'd ever seen it. Beth felt as if she could see the whole Pacific Ocean as she drove down the coast. The roadside was bright with California poppies, and the thought of going back to Maine, where it was basically still the dead of winter, left a bad taste in her mouth.

What if she didn't go back?

What if she stayed?

She had no idea how she might make that happen, but she realized that she *wanted* to. She didn't want to go crawling back home in defeat. She wanted this California adventure that she had promised herself.

But the thought of going it alone absolutely terrified her.

Beth parked in the small parking lot next to the yarn store just before eight o'clock. The door was unlocked, and she let herself in.

"You're here bright and early," Yolanda said with approval. "Is that one of yours?"

"What?" Beth asked blankly.

"The sweater. Did you make it?"

"Oh. Yes. I did."

"And what did you make with the scrap yarn I gave you?"

"Nothing yet," Beth admitted. She had completely forgotten about the previous day's homework. "Yesterday was... hard."

"What happened?" Yolanda asked.

Beth looked down at the warped wooden floor. "My boyfriend dumped me."

"Is that all?"

Beth looked up at the old lady in surprise. She couldn't help but grin at the look of exasperation on Yolanda's face.

"Young men are a dime a dozen," the owner of the yarn store told her. "And if he doesn't value you, it's good riddance to bad rubbish. Another will come along soon enough."

"I'm not sure if I'll be able to stay here," Beth said. "The lease on the apartment in Half Moon Bay is in his name. He left for a few days to give me time to decide what I'm going to do, but if I don't find a new place to live by the end of this week, I'll have to go home and stay with my mom for a while. I don't have enough saved up for a hotel or anything."

Beth didn't want to say as much, but she doubted that this job would pay for a rental, never mind a hotel room. Minimum wage in California was a bit higher than in Maine, but the cost of rent was jaw-dropping. Beth had done a cursory search online in the wee hours of the morning, only to discover that a tiny studio would cost her three weeks wages... and that's assuming that Yolanda needed somebody to work full-time.

Beth's potential employer was looking at her with a thoughtful expression. "Do you *want* to stay?"

Beth considered that question for a moment, remembering her bobcat encounter with sudden clarity. She had spent weeks poring over articles on California, reading about Yosemite Valley and Sequoia National Park. As Yolanda waited patiently for an answer, Beth thought about the rolling fields of the strawberry farm she had driven past that morning on the way to Redwood Grove, about the vast expanse of forest and wide sandy beaches and all of the places she had yet to explore. She realized with a jolt of surprise that this was *exactly* where she wanted to be... Josh or no Josh.

"I do," Beth said firmly. "Yes."

"Then follow me." Yolanda snatched up a wooden cane from under the counter and led Beth to the back of the store. She undid a latch, and one of the yarn-packed shelves swung forward to reveal a hidden door, which in turn opened to reveal a narrow old staircase. Yolanda made her way up the stairs slowly, one ponderous step at a time, and Beth followed.

Upstairs was a small, beautiful one-bedroom apartment. The front windows overlooked Main Street, and the view out the back window was green with pine needles. It had a few bits of furniture - a small dining set in the main room, a metal bed with mattress and chest of drawers in the pint-sized bedroom - and a round little refrigerator that was probably several decades older than Beth. When she opened it, though, it was perfectly cold, with a beckoning little lightbulb that just begged for fresh produce to shine on.

"This place is so beautiful," Beth breathed reverently.

"I lived here for twenty-two years," Yolanda said. "I would live here still, but my old knees can't take going up and down the stairs all day. My son built me my own little home on his land just a mile outside of town, and I moved there a few months ago. I never listed this place because I didn't want just anyone coming through my shop every day."

"I don't think I would be able to pay you what this place is worth," Beth said, even as she looked around the beautiful little apartment with a growing sense of longing.

"You can pay me a deposit," Yolanda told her. "After that, it's yours."

Beth turned to stare at her. "I don't understand."

"As long as you're working here in the shop, you can live up above. I need someone to work six days a week, six hours a day. Minimum wage, plus free rent. You'll have Mondays off. Does that sound agreeable?"

"That sounds amazing," Beth said. She felt sure that her mom would help with the deposit so that Beth could use her meager savings for bedding and kitchen stuff. A place of her own... Beth could barely wrap her head around it, but her heart felt like the clouds had parted and let down the year's first beam of golden summer sunshine.

"Good. Then come downstairs and I'll show you how I do inventory."

"Thank you! Thank you so much."

Yolanda waved away her thanks. "I am long overdue for retirement, and no one wants to put in an honest day's work anymore. I don't want to train an endless line of people who will only work a few hours a week. I want to train *one* person, and then I want to spend my days at home with my grandchildren. Do you think you can manage this place, Beth?"

Running a register and ordering yarn? Talking about knitting all day long? Beth grinned. "I do."

"Then let's get started." Yolanda gestured to the stairs. "I suppose I should let you go down first. You'll find a half-finished shawl under the counter. It will go in the front window when it's finished. See what sort of progress you can make on it by the time I make it safely down the stairs."

Beth's grin broadened, and she headed down the stairs two at a time.

6

Ava

WHEN SHE LEFT the hospital after two nights in that horrible plastic chair, Ava cut through Redwood Grove on her way to Gran's house. Her grandmother being stuck in the hospital wasn't something that Ava could control, but she could at least make sure that her grandmother never had to eat another bite of hospital food. Toni had delivered more than enough broth and soup and tea to last Gran today and tonight, and the nurses had okayed Ava bringing back some solid food when she returned the next morning.

The name had changed, but Redwood Grove's single grocery store was much the same as it has been when Ava was growing up. There were some new bougie products, but the produce section and the butcher's counter were just as she remembered them. It was comforting and disorienting all at once.

Ava moved woodenly through the store, sleep deprived and grief stricken. She just wanted to load up on the basics and get out before she saw anyone that she knew.

But this was Redwood Grove, and that was easier said than done.

"Avalon! It is so wonderful to see you. How is your grandmother?" Ava got a general impression of flowing cotton clothes in shades of orange and purple before she turned back to the hill of oranges that dominated the produce section. Like Redwood Grove itself, Echo Murray never seemed to change.

"Hello, Echo," Ava said tiredly. "Gran is fine."

That was an outright lie, but what else could she do? Tell the most talkative woman in town about Gran's foot right there in the middle of the grocery store? Everyone was sure to find out eventually, but Ava intended to stem the tide of well-meaning busybodies if she could.

"Is she still in the hospital?" Echo pressed.

"She is. I'm not sure for how much longer. I'm just buying some groceries to make her some food for when I go back tomorrow." Ava turned away. But Echo, as usual, could not take a hint.

"Your aura is terribly dingy." The slender, white-haired woman began pinching at the air around Ava's head, as if clearing the cobwebs from her energetic field. Ava looked at her, wide-eyed, but Echo just went on cleaning the air.

"You're approaching a time of great change, dear heart. What you have been avoiding all of your life is coming toward you, and quicker than you would like. I see a dark cloud hanging over you, and I don't just mean the fear and guilt that cling to you today. There's a storm brewing."

"Echo, I don't have the energy for this today."

"Don't worry, Avalon," Echo said brightly. She shook out her hands and then reached up to touch Ava's cheek. As exasperating as Echo generally was, there was something deeply soothing in her touch. Simply seeing a familiar face was comforting, but it was more than that. Echo's loving expression gave Ava the same feeling that visiting Gran at Hoffman Farm always had. In that moment, she felt like a child being tucked under a homemade quilt, warm and safe. "Storms clear the air and water the ground. You'll be better off when the storm has passed. Just you wait and see. The best years of your life are yet to come."

The best years of Ava's life were behind her, those early years with her precious babies, but she didn't bother arguing. She accepted a hug from Echo, made it out of the store without encountering any other characters from her childhood, and then drove down the winding mountain road to Gran's farm.

As Ava drove out of the forest, the view over the hills to the distant ocean horizon brought a rush of nostalgia. Her chest was so full of joy and grief at the same time that it threatened to overwhelm her. Long lines of green strawberry plants dotted with white flowers stretched out across the rolling hills of Hoffman Farm. Flowers blossomed on the ninety-year-old apple trees around the little two-story house that had stood there for over a century.

In some ways, Ava's childhood home never changed.

But not everything was the same. On the other side of the acreage, the workers' cabins shone with a fresh coat of whitewash. The wooden cabins back behind the fields had been falling down when Ava was young, not fit for human habitation. But Gran had fixed them up about twenty years ago to provide free housing for migrant workers, and more recently her farm manager had renovated them to provide permanent homes for some of the people who worked at Hoffman farm.

"It means their children will be able to go to school here," Gran had told her over the phone, "and our workers won't have to commute three hours a day to some inland town where the rents aren't sky high. Wait until you see the cabins, Ava. They're so cozy that I'm tempted to move into one myself and rent out the farmhouse. I just might, too."

The more that Gran sang Nolan's praises, the more that Ava resisted coming home. She had been to visit a handful of times since Gran had hired her high school sweetheart as farm manager, but each time, she had gotten in and out without seeing him. Ava had wanted to be furious with her grandmother for hiring the boy who had broken her heart so long ago, but she just couldn't find it in her to be angry with Gran for anything. Her decisions often seemed a little odd on the outside, but they were always for the best – or at the very least, they were made with the best of intentions.

Gran had told her more than once how much she wanted Ava and Nolan to spend some time together. But Ava had always put her off. Whoever Nolan was now, he was a stranger to her – and the memories that he dredged up were just too painful to face. Besides, her time with Gran and Toni (and her kids, when they could be persuaded to visit the farm with her) was too precious to squander.

She wondered now why their time together had been in such short supply. It was a nine-hour drive, not an international flight or an ocean voyage. She should have made more time for her aging grandmother. And as she walked around the farm now, Ava was reminded that not all of the recent changes had been positive.

The farm store and café that had been the center point of Ava's childhood was shuttered. The effort that Gran had put into keeping it open just hadn't been worth it anymore; in its final years, she had spent more money to have someone tend the store than she'd made from the sales. Ava hadn't felt more than a slight twinge of regret when Gran had told her over the phone that she was closing the place, but seeing it all shut it up today was... different, somehow.

"Ava!" Nolan rounded the corner and walked toward her with long strides. "Did you just come from the hospital?"

The sight of him took her breath away. It was the first time in decades that she had seen her high school sweetheart... other than that brief meeting in the hospital room, dimly lit and blurred by a haze of guilt and fear for Gran. Now, in the sunshine, it was all that she could do to keep herself from staring slack-jawed at her first love.

Nolan had always been tall... but had he been *this* tall? Ava didn't think that it was her imagination; he had grown at least a couple of inches since he was seventeen. And he had only gotten more handsome, which was an added thorn in a wound that had never healed. Nolan's jaw was stronger now than it had been and covered with a dark shadow of stubble. His teal-green eyes were just the same, and his auburn hair was as thick and dark as ever.

Damn him. It was a solid thirty seconds before Ava managed to string a handful of words together.

"By way of Wild Roots, yeah. I wanted to make her some food before I go back tomorrow."

"How is she?" He stood a scant foot away from her, and she took a step back.

"Gran is doing well, thank you," Ava said, hating how stilted and awkward she sounded. "She finished the chicken broth you brought and Toni's nettle soup." She didn't have the heart to tell him how much pain Gran had been in when the medication in her blood started to wear thin, or how wan and helpless she had looked in that huge hospital bed after the warm soup and fresh pain meds had sent her into a deep sleep mid-morning.

"Having an appetite is a great sign," Nolan told her. How could he talk to her as if she were just another acquaintance? As if they had never meant anything to each other? Ava's stomach churned with a mix of emotions that she was too tired to untangle.

"Were you able to speak with her doctors?" he asked.

"Yes," Ava said haltingly, "I was able to run one of them down late this morning. He told me that there's no sign of the infection that was in danger of going septic, and that her vital signs are as good as he might expect to see from someone half her age recovering from that type of surgery."

Nolan's face lit up with relief. "So she's going to be okay."

"It's a long road to recovery, but yeah." Ava smiled at him as she let hope fill her chest with warmth. "I think she is."

Someone shouted questions from the field, and Nolan turned away and responded in rapid-fire Spanish. The sudden reminder of how little she knew this man felt like a slap to the face. The boy that Ava had loved hadn't spoken any Spanish at all – he'd been impressed by Ava's rudimentary attempts when he'd moved to California at fifteen – and the man in front of her was completely fluent. When had he learned? *Where* had he learned?

She could get the gist of a conversation, but her Spanish wasn't good enough to understand everything that was said. From what she could tell, Nolan's Spanish was effortless, and his accent seemed to be flawless. And Ava's grasp of the language aside, there was no mistaking easy comfort of his tone. She got the feeling that Nolan was the sort of boss who could joke with his employees – and let them crack jokes at his expense. Like they shared a mutual respect.

Ava gave herself a mental kick to the butt. She was already exhausted, and these mental gymnastics weren't going to help anything. It didn't matter where Nolan had learned Spanish. It didn't matter what sort of boss he was, so long as Gran could count on him. Ava needed to focus.

Nolan turned back to her with an easy smile and asked, "Are you headed back to the hospital this evening? You're welcome to ride with me. To save on gas," he added, rubbing a hand over the back of his sun-browned neck.

"I was planning to go back first thing tomorrow morning," Ava replied. She felt a fresh wash of shame at the idea of leaving Gran overnight, but she was in desperate need of some real sleep before she drove that narrow mountain road and high-traffic highway again.

"Just as well. If we split up our visits, she won't need to spend too much time alone." He glanced over at a truck that sat idling nearby and said, "They're waiting on me. We need to start harvesting for tomorrow's market. I'll be around. Call or text if you need anything."

"Thank you," Ava said, but Nolan was already jogging over to the truck. She watched him go, admiring the breadth of his shoulders beneath the sun-bleached fabric of his cotton work shirt. Then she snapped back to reality and went inside to make herself a fresh pot of coffee.

The little house was stuffy and dim. Being there without Gran made Ava's heart ache, and she tried to ignore the pervasive guilt of not being by her grandmother's side every minute of the day. At least here, there was productive work to be done. As her coffee brewed, Ava opened up all of the windows of Gran's little wooden house. She cleaned the wilted spinach out of the fridge and started a fresh pot of chicken soup. Then she got to cleaning.

As she worked her way from the wood-beam ceilings to the creaky wooden floor, Ava realized that her grandmother had started to struggle with the upkeep of her home. Gran's fierce independence had always seemed like more of a strength than a weakness, but Ava could see how that independent streak had led Gran to trouble. She hadn't sought help when the infection in her leg went beyond what she could handle with her tinctures and salves. And she hadn't asked for help when the upkeep of her house became too much for her.

The dust on top of the cabinets was thick. Ava had such vivid memories of her grandmother standing on chairs and climbing up on her kitchen counter every Saturday afternoon to make sure that her house was spotless, and the realization that Gran was far too old to be doing that anymore hit Ava in the gut.

Gran was eighty-three years old. Of course she couldn't climb up on the kitchen counters to clean the tops of her cabinets. And it was no surprise that she hadn't brought anyone in to do it for her. Ava should have seen this coming.

She should have known that Gran would need more help. She should have visited more often and hired a housekeeper over whatever fight her grandmother would doubtlessly have put up.

But she had neglected her grandmother. She had allowed her childish belief that her grandmother was eternal and invincible to cloud her judgment. She had let her ridiculous fears over seeing Nolan again keep her away from the farm. And she had gotten here far too late to save Gran from major surgery and an excruciating recovery.

But she was here now. And she would do everything that she could to ensure that her grandmother made it back to her home safe and sound.

Ava's brain was in overdrive as she rolled out the crust for Gran's favorite apple-strawberry pie. Bringing Gran food and seeing her home from the hospital was one thing. But how was she going to ensure that Gran was well cared for in her golden years? Ava wasn't sure how she was going to make ends meet during this long stay, never mind paying for in-home care once she had gone home to San Diego.

As she looked out the kitchen window toward the sad, shuttered back door of the old café, the seed of an idea began to germinate.

She could get the café and farm store running again. The place had been a cornerstone of Hoffman Farm once, and it could be again. How many tourists and commuters drove past every day? This place was prime real estate, and it was going to waste. With a grand opening this summer and the right staff, the café could generate enough profits to pay for round-the-clock care for Gran for as long as she needed it.

And Ava could make that happen. She had gotten

distracted and had let her grandmother down, but she could still make it up to her. By some miracle, Margaret Hoffman was going to pull through. The doctor had told Ava that there was every reason to believe that her grandmother would regain full mobility. There had been a flood of information on physical therapy and prosthetics that Ava had been too exhausted to take in completely, but that had been the gist of it. Gran was recovering, and she would walk again. Eventually.

And when she finally came home from the hospital, it would be to a clean house and a thriving café. The revived business would cover the cost of a home nurse, a housekeeper, and a cook, whatever Gran needed to see her through her golden years in style.

Ava would see to it that her grandmother never set foot in a hospital again...no matter what it took.

7

Toni

"You hitchhiked?" Toni exclaimed. "Juniper, that's not safe!"

Juniper gave her a sardonic little smile as she wiped tear-streaked mascara from her cheeks. "Did you or did you not hitchhike from Argentina to Mexico as a teenager?"

Damn it. Toni should have known that those stories would come back to bite her.

"I was *nineteen*," she said, as if that made a difference to her sixteen-year-old niece. "And mostly I took buses."

"And donkeys?" Juniper teased, smiling at her aunt even as fresh tears streamed down her face.

"The occasional llama," Toni said, deadpan. "Things were different back then."

Juniper laughed through her tears and then wiped them away.

"We should call your dad," Toni said quietly.

"He has enough to deal with today." The light went out of Juniper's eyes, and Toni could *see* her retreating back into herself. "Enough to worry about."

"He'll be worried about *you* if the school calls him."

Juniper shrugged and turned away.

"All jokes aside," Toni told her, "hitchhiking alone isn't okay. It's not safe, and it's not... *you*. What were you thinking?"

"I wasn't thinking." Juniper's voice was halting and stilted, like she'd tried so hard to compartmentalize her feelings that it had broken her. "I found her in the bathroom this morning, and Dad drove her back to rehab. That new center she likes, the one over the hill?"

Toni felt a sudden rage at Juniper's parents. They had failed her over and over again. Her mother was one thing; Toni didn't know what monsters that woman was dealing with that had her relapsing time and again. But for Ethan to keep letting that woman back into his daughter's life, into their *home*, was just inexcusable. But that was a conversation that Toni would have with her brother another time. Her anger had no place in the here and now. She took a deep breath and reached out to put a hand on her niece's shoulder.

"I'm sorry that your morning was so brutally hard. You could've called me, Juniper. I would've come and picked you up. But hitchhiking alone..."

Juniper's eyes were distant as she looked out over the garden. "I tried to go to school. I didn't want to be home alone, so I just walked to school. I walked into my first classroom, and I sat down... and I realized that there was no way I was going to be able to focus today. So I told my AP

Psych teacher what had happened, and I walked right back out again. She was really nice about it.

"I left all of my school stuff in my locker, and I just started walking. I went down to West Cliff and walked all the way to the end. I was just going to go to Natural Bridges and put my feet in the sand. Clear my head. But then... I just kept walking. For a few hours, I guess. Somewhere along the One, a woman pulled over and asked if I needed a ride. So I asked her to bring me here. It was way out of her way, I think, but she did it."

"Well, that was nice of her," Toni said flatly. It didn't do to think of what *could* have happened to her beautiful young niece. It seemed to Toni that people were mostly good – even good enough to go out of their way to give a young girl a ride to a safe haven. She was grateful for that. "But next time, I want you to call me. No matter where you are or what I'm doing, I'll come get you."

"Next time she relapses?" Juniper said in a low, quiet voice.

Toni's heart broke all over again. "Next time you need help, Junebug. For any reason."

Juniper shrugged and turned away. She walked toward the borage plants and plucked a star-shaped flower without touching the prickly stems.

"I don't wanna go back to school, Nia."

"You don't have to go to school today," Toni told her. "It would be past the end of the school day by the time we got down there anyway. I'll make some tea, and we'll–"

"I don't want to go back to school ever," Juniper said.

Toni put an arm around Juniper's shoulders and looked

out over the garden. They were quiet for a while, listening to birdsong and the hum of the bees.

"That's a decision for another day," she said after a while. "Why don't you come inside and have some tea?"

Juniper nodded and followed Toni inside. She browsed through the overflowing bookshelves that dominated the little living room while Toni brewed them each a cup of tea. When it was ready, Toni settled Juniper in a patch of sunlight and pressed the mug into her hands.

"This is good," she said after her first cautious sip. "What is it?"

"Lemon balm," Toni said distractedly. "Nettle. Chamomile. A bit of hops and my milky oat tincture. Some local honey." She checked her phone. "Juniper, one of us needs to call your dad before the school does. Or at least text him."

Wordlessly, Juniper handed over her phone. The screen was filled with grocery requests on her side and one *I'll be home late today* from her dad. At the bottom, a text from Juniper read, *Left school early and got a ride to Redwood Grove. Staying at Nia's tonight.*

"Good enough," Toni approved, handing the phone back. "Thank you."

Juniper nodded and sipped at her tea. Toni wanted desperately to pull her niece out of her shell and see her smile, maybe even hear her laugh, but it was too soon for that. Juniper needed more time to process what had happened this morning. It was enough that she was here safe. So Toni just stood, kissed Juniper on the head, and went to load up her dehydrators with calendula flowers.

A text message came in from Ava while she worked. It

was a picture of two homemade pies and the caption, *One for Gran and one for us. Can you come over?*

When Toni went back into the living room with a second cup of tea and a plate of Juniper's favorite lemon-ginger cookies, her niece was poring over a stack of books on herbalism. It warmed Toni's heart to see it, and she was filled with a sudden certainty that Juniper was going to be okay.

"Ava's in town," Toni told her as she set the tea and cookies on the coffee table. "She invited me over for pie. Do you want to come?"

Juniper looked up from the books. "To Gran's house?"

Gran was nearly as dear to Juniper as she was to Toni. Juniper had never known her maternal grandmother, and Toni's stepmother gave off all the warmth of a marble statue. Gran had filled in, especially in Juniper's early years when she and Ethan still lived in Redwood Grove. Toni could still see her five-year-old niece standing on a stool in Gran's kitchen, lustrous brown hair down to her waist, staring enraptured at Gran as she peeled an entire apple in one long spiral.

"Yeah, Ava's at Hoffman Farm." Toni sat down on the couch and said, "Gran's in the hospital."

"What?" Juniper sat up with a start, and the book she'd been looking at drifted shut. "Why? What's wrong with her?"

"She had an infection in her foot, and her leg," Toni said carefully, holding back the worst of it. "I think she'll be okay, but she's been really sick. It was a shock to Ava, and I want to make sure she's all right. Do you want to come? She made pie."

Juniper picked up her fresh mug of tea and held it in both

hands. Looking down into the golden liquid, she said, "I just want to curl up and read for a while, if that's okay."

"That's fine," Toni assured her. "I won't be gone long."

Juniper looked up at her, clear brown eyes warm and sincere. "I do want to go see Gran, though. Next time you visit her in the hospital?"

Toni squeezed her hand. "Gran would love that."

Nolan was loading a truck with produce when Toni drove onto Gran's property, and she waved at him as she headed up the dirt road. He flashed her a grin and greeted her with a dramatic bow. Toni laughed and pulled up next to his truck.

"How are you?" Toni asked over the rumble of her truck's engine.

"It's been a phenomenal spring." The cheerful non-answer didn't surprise her. No man Toni had ever met would have responded to a casual *how are you* with an honest, *Well, I'm terrified for our matriarch, and seeing the girl that I was head-over-heels in love with as a kid for the first time in decades has brought up a lot of confusing emotions.* So Toni just smiled and nodded.

And to be fair, it *was* a phenomenal spring. They'd gotten plenty of rain that winter, and the central coast was more lush and verdant than Toni had seen it in years. Her garden was exploding with blooms and bees, and even the roadsides were a riot of color lately.

"Are you working the market this Saturday?" she asked him.

"Come rain or shine."

"I'll see you then." Toni drove on, reflecting on how

strange this ill-timed reunion must be for him and Ava. The three of them – Toni and Ava and Nolan – had been inseparable at fifteen. The three amigos. Toni had befriended Nolan first, the new kid in her marine biology class, and immediately roped him into lunches with her and her bestie. Ava had gone starry-eyed immediately. And Toni had encouraged them, had been the go-between encouraging her two shy friends to take the leap and go on that first date, doubling with her and her then-boyfriend. Before long, Nolan and Ava were inseparable. Or they seemed to be. And then it had ended the way that it ended. And Toni had never understood why. One minute Ava and Nolan were planning their life together, travel and farm work and kids... and then he was gone.

Nolan had left town as soon as they graduated without even staying for the ceremony. Like Toni, he had spent nearly twenty years traveling the world before coming back to roost in Redwood Grove. After he left, Ava had holed up at Gran's house and mourned all summer before finally going to San Diego for college... only to drop out and marry a military man ten years her senior and not remotely her type. Toni had to watch her best friend endure two decades of an increasingly miserable marriage, tempered by the joy that she found in motherhood. It had been a relief when Ava finally left the man who took her for granted, but Toni was still waiting for her best friend to get the light back in her eyes. She had been so beaten down for so long that even now that she was free, she was living half of a life. Still working in the same restaurant, living in a rental that she didn't really love... living a *life* that she didn't really love.

And of course, this hideously stressful ordeal that Gran

was going through hadn't helped in the slightest. Not yet, at least. Maybe it would serve as the wakeup call that Ava so desperately needed. Maybe it would bring Toni's best friend home again... for good this time.

Toni found Ava sitting at Gran's kitchen table. The entire surface of the wide farmhouse table was covered in papers. There were bills and pay stubs and bank statements... even ledgers that went back several decades. Ava hardly glanced up at Toni when she walked in, so Toni set about cutting them each a slice of the pie that Ava had made.

"Up," she ordered once their food was plated. Toni's hands were full, so she tapped Ava's hip with one leather-clad foot.

Ava looked up at her in surprise. "What did you say?"

"Pie. Porch. March."

Ava chuckled and followed Toni out onto Gran's front porch. They each sat on one of the weathered wooden chairs and watched the late afternoon sunlight glinting off of the ocean. Before they touched their food, though, a beat-up old Cadillac came bumping up the dirt road.

Echo parked right at the bottom of the porch steps and climbed out of her car with a huge casserole dish tucked under her arm.

"Toni! Aren't you a sight for sore eyes? You're radiant."

"Thank you, Echo." Toni went to greet her and then bent to kiss the old lady on the cheek.

Echo smiled, shaking her head in wonder. "You're looking positively golden, dear heart."

"What's this?" Toni asked as she took the casserole dish from Echo's hands.

"Chicken enchiladas for Marge. They're her favorite."

"That's lovely. Thank you so much."

Echo looked up at Ava, and immediately her expression clouded over. She put a hand to her forehead as if in pain, and Toni looked between the two of them with a tremor of worry. "What? What is it?"

"There's a cloud hanging over her, dear one," Echo said.

"What does that mean?"

But Echo just shook her head. "I've said too much already." Her expression brightened as she looked up at Toni and said, "You'll stand by her, won't you?"

"Always."

Echo reached up to pat her on the cheek. "You were always a good girl. Tell Marge I said hello."

She hopped into her car and drove off without another word. Toni shook her head and trotted back up the porch steps to drop Echo's offering in the kitchen. Then she went back outside to reclaim her slice of apple-strawberry pie.

"This pie is delicious," Toni said after her first bite.

"Almost as good as Gran's," Ava agreed.

"I can't believe there are strawberries already."

"There aren't. Not here, at least. These are from the grocery store."

"Gran would be horrified," Toni joked.

"The apples were from the root cellar." Ava's voice tried and failed to hit a cheerful note. She took another bite of her pie, looking glum. They had been friends long enough that Toni could guess what Ava was thinking. She had wanted to make sure that she made Gran's favorite pie... whether or not she made it home for strawberry season. They finished their food in silence, watching cars move up and down the coastal highway.

"What did the doctors say?" Toni asked at last.

"Seems like she's going to pull through," Ava said, "but even when she's released from the hospital, she'll probably have to spend several months in recovery. Extended care facility, I think they called it."

"She'll hate that," Toni murmured. "She'll say it's for old people."

"I know it. I'm trying to figure out how to bring her straight home."

"It's a kind thought, Ava, but she's going to need round-the-clock care for a long time. Octogenarians can be slow to heal."

"Her finances are a mess," Ava acknowledged. "She pays her workers well, but there's nothing left for her. The farm isn't turning enough of a profit to support her. She's been living off savings for years. And I can't afford in-home care. Her insurance won't cover a halfway decent nursing home. I can't put her in one of those places, Toni. She's not going to get her strength back if she hears that's where she's headed next."

She'd rather be buried under the apple trees, Toni thought.

"So I've decided to reopen the café. Pie, strawberry shortcake, jam. Strawberry lemonade. Just like when we were kids. We already have the space. And I can run it myself until I have the money to hire someone. My savings may not cover a nurse, but I have enough to spruce the place up a bit."

"It's a good idea. But Ava," she cautioned, "it could be a long time before the café turns a profit again. It could sustain Gran long-term, but it's not an immediate solution."

"Then I'll do more," Ava insisted. "You-pick days for families, like Gran used to do when we were little. A farm stand on the highway. A whole big fundraising event if I have to. The town will turn up for Gran. You know they will."

Now *that* idea had legs. "They would," Toni agreed. "We all would. But how long can you stay? What about your job?"

Ava swatted her questions away. "My job will take me back no matter how long I stay away. I've been there for years. And my friend Isela found someone to sublet my house for the next two months. If I stay longer than that, it will be easy to rent it out as a vacation home this summer."

"It'll be nice having you home for a while." Toni reached out and took Ava's hand. "I'll help however I can."

Tears rose to Ava's eyes, but she gave Toni a genuine smile. "Thank you."

"I'm sorry that I didn't check in on her more often," Toni said as her guilt rose to the surface. "I should have, but I just get so crazy busy that the weeks flash by before I even have time to straighten up and look around. It feels like everyone in my family is barely treading water, me included."

"I know the feeling." Ava squeezed Toni's hand. "You don't have anything to be sorry for. If it's anyone's fault, it's mine."

"Don't say that. What could you have done?"

"I could have been here. Maggie's in Portland and Ryan's at his dad's house six nights out of seven. I don't have any excuse to stay away as long as I have."

"You had your work, your life."

"Some life," Ava muttered cryptically. "And my work is flexible. From now on, I'm going to visit at least once a month. And I'm going to find someone amazing to take care of Gran before I go."

"It's a good plan," Toni told her. "Gran's lucky to have you."

"*We*'re lucky to have *her*."

"This was a powerful reminder not to take her for granted, that's for sure."

"I was so scared," Ava admitted with a crack in her voice.

"Me too. But Gran's a fighter. We'll celebrate her hundredth birthday right here. You'll see."

Ava nodded. "I sure hope so."

8

Ava

Ava closed her car door and stretched. Her back was stiff and sore from the long drive to the hospital and back. She'd had a nice catch-up session with her daughter on her way home – or rather, on the drive back to Hoffman Farm – but the drive *to* the hospital that morning had been two excruciating hours of worry. If Ava was going to keep doing this every day – and she did intend to keep visiting daily for as long as her grandmother was in the hospital – she would need to stock up on audiobooks to occupy her mind on the long, winding drive through the mountains.

"Ava!"

Nolan's voice made her jump, and she held one hand over her fluttering heart as she turned to face him. He was walking up the farm's private dirt road with a pack of admirers hot on his heels: four farm dogs plus a significant number of resident chickens and one jealous rooster. As he passed Gran's house, a fat orange cat streaked down the stairs to join the parade.

The farm manager looked like he had been out in the fields all morning. His faded blue jeans were dusted with compost, and when he removed his hat, there was an endearing circle imprinted in his thick auburn hair. The orange cat pressed against his legs as he came to a stop in front of Ava, and he reached down absentmindedly to scratch its head.

"How's Gran today?" he asked. His vibrant eyes, more blue than green this morning, were intent on her face. For a moment, Ava was struck dumb. She turned her attention to the elderly pit bull that was pawing at her foot, and she scratched the old girl's head for a moment while she found her voice.

"She's in surprisingly good spirits. It seems that the hospital isn't exactly the torture chamber that she was expecting. The nurses dote on her. She was even able to eat a couple of slices of pie."

"I'm glad to hear it," Nolan said in a tone of deep relief. "She was so subdued when I went by last night... I'm not used to carrying the conversation when we talk. But it was late in the day. I was hoping that she was just tired."

Ava nodded, still looking down at the dogs as the other three vied for her attention. The young golden retriever mix nearly knocked her off balance, and she laughed unsteadily as her behind bumped into the door of her car.

"Phoenix, sit," Nolan ordered. The dog obeyed immediately, though he still managed to inch forward until he could nose Ava's hand. She grinned and scratched his ears.

"Phoenix?" she asked, glancing up at Nolan.

"He was half dead when Gran found him. Hardly had any hair on him at all. But she turned him around quick and gave him that name when his golden coat started growing back in."

Ava nodded as she bent down to scratch the thick fur on Phoenix's chest. "I remember now. He was so pathetic the last time I was here, just a bald little lump tucked into a dog bed by the wood stove. I wouldn't have recognized him."

"Your grandmother can work miracles," Nolan said softly. The tone of his voice pierced Ava's heart, and she kept her eyes on the dogs.

"I know. I can't even tell you how many orphaned kittens and injured birds I brought her when I was a little girl. A surprising number of them pulled through – more than anyone else would have managed, I think. Gran gave each little creature her all... but when they didn't pull through, she was still always so calm and composed. We would bury them out under the apple trees, or put them beneath that year's tomato starts, and she'd move on with her day."

"Any true farmer becomes comfortable with death sooner or later," Nolan said.

Ava nodded thoughtfully, looking over at the chickens that scratched in the dirt nearby. "When I was a little girl, it baffled me how Gran could spend hours caring for an injured hen and then go out in the yard and kill a young rooster for the soup pot."

"She is large," Nolan murmured, smiling as he scratched Phoenix's head. "She contains multitudes."

Ava's heart twisted again, and she pushed down a slew of memories that threatened to surface. "Are you quoting Whitman?"

"Paraphrasing," Nolan said with an apologetic shrug. Then he looked up at her and grinned. "Are you surprised? 'Keep your face always towards the sunshine.' He's the farmer's poet if there ever was one."

"Dismiss whatever insults your own soul," Ava quoted, looking Nolan in the eyes. God, the pull she felt toward him was as strong as it had ever been. And just in that moment, Ava didn't want to resist it.

He smiled, holding her gaze. "Exactly."

His hand brushed hers as they both reached to pet Gran's old hound dog at the same moment. Shock sparked through Ava's fingers, and she straightened up so quickly that she felt a bit lightheaded.

She was playing with fire. How dare he speak to her as if he hadn't dropped her in the dirt the moment they were done with high school? How could she let herself be taken in by that charming smile? If he hadn't cared for her enough to stay by her side when they were young, he couldn't possibly be interested in a woman several months older than he was. He probably had a thirty-year-old girlfriend. Girlfriends. His charm was indiscriminate, probably even unconscious, and Ava wouldn't let herself be taken in by it. Not again.

"I should go," she muttered, still looking down at the dogs.

"No worries," Nolan said easily. "I should get back to work. There's still a lot to do before market day tomorrow."

"Thank you, Nolan," Ava said, trying to speak to him the way she would speak to any other worker managing Gran's farm. "I know it's a comfort to her that you're here running things."

Nolan nodded his acknowledgement and walked back

down the road, animals at his heels. The old hound dog and the pit bull stayed with Ava, tails thumping in the shade of her car.

Ava caught herself watching Nolan as he walked down the road and tore her eyes away with a muttered curse. He was just another employee. Just a boy that she'd known in high school. She had more important things to do than admire the way that the farm manager carried himself.

The key to the old café was just where Gran told her it would be, and Ava set to work. She had only been at it long enough to open the windows and kick up several years' worth of dust when she felt someone watching her.

"Who are you?"

Ava looked up to see a small girl of six or seven standing in the doorway. Two sleek black braids hung past the front pocket of her purple overalls. Ava smiled at her, but the girl continued to peer at her with narrow-eyed suspicion.

"No one's supposed to be in here. Gran closed it."

"Gran gave me the key so I can fix it up for her. Then we can give her a big party when she's well enough to come home."

"Will there be lemonade?" the girl asked. "Gran loves lemonade."

"Definitely. My name is Ava. What's yours?"

"Lucia."

"Pleased to meet you, Lucia."

Ava heard Lucia's mother before she saw her. She called to Lucia in a liquid rush of Spanish that Ava barely caught a word of. When she stepped into the café, she nodded to Ava in greeting, then took in the dusty interior and wrinkled her nose.

"I told her about the party," Lucia chirped.

"The party is just step one of my plan," Ava confided. "Step two is to get the café running again. We'll have to bake lots and lots of pies."

Lucia said something to her mother and then translated for her back to Ava. "Mami says that it's a good plan, and lots of people will come here."

Ava smiled at Lucia's mother and introduced herself.

"I'm Marisol," the woman said in turn. *"¿Puedo ayudarte?"*

"I'm pleased to meet you, Marisol. And thank you for the offer, but please don't feel obligated."

"We want to help," Marisol replied. *"¿No hablas español?"*

"I do speak a bit of Spanish," Ava said apologetically, "but I can understand more than I speak."

"We make it work." Marisol responded with a smile before saying something to Lucia and heading outside.

"She went to get some things to help you clean. For Gran."

"Oh, she doesn't have to do that."

"She wants to help Gran," Lucia said earnestly. "We all do."

Ava smiled at the little girl. "That's very kind."

Marisol returned with a box of trash bags and two buckets full of cleaning supplies, trailed by a blond girl in her twenties whom Ava had never seen before. Her corn-silk hair was pulled into a tight bun, and her slender body was swallowed up by the oversized coveralls that she wore.

"Hey," Ava greeted her. "I'm Ava."

The young woman nodded without lifting her gaze from

the floor. How many people had passed through the farm over Ava's lifetime? More than she could count – and yet Gran remembered each one by name, and she could tell their whole story decades later.

Ava was just one of many lost souls that Gran had taken in over the years. A child Gran had practically raised as her own when Ava's own parents had cast her off. Gran had done the same thing for Toni, more or less, and for so many others. Ava's mother, Gran's daughter Lyra, had always resented the constant flow of people whom she saw as competing for her mother's love and attention. But Ava had never minded the extra family that ebbed and flowed around her. It had made her childhood with Gran exciting, turning their little family of two into something so much richer.

With Gran in the hospital, the wheel of Hoffman Farm had lost its axis. But Ava wouldn't let it fall to the wayside; she would keep the wheel turning until Gran was safely home.

The three women made quick work of the dusty front room of the café. The neglected kitchen would take longer, but they made good headway there too. Lucia flitted from one woman to another like a songbird, and her steady chatter kept Ava's spirits up.

It was a few hours before the young woman with the cornsilk hair – she'd heard Lucia call her Greta – felt ready to say something to Ava. When she did speak, her voice was surprisingly low and melodious. Her tone, on the other hand, was unsurprisingly timid. Her whole presence felt nervously apologetic in a way that hurt Ava's heart.

"We tried to help Miss Hoffman however we could, but you know how independent she is."

"She's stubborn," Ava agreed. She looked up from the stovetop that she was scrubbing to smile at Greta. "I'm glad she had all of you to help. I just wish I'd come to visit more often."

"We had to get sneaky," Greta said with a lightning-flash smile. Her eyes were on the grout of the tile floor as she scrubbed at it with a bristle brush, and Ava had to crouch down in front of her to catch everything that she was saying. "Lucia and I would weed the garden when Gran went to town, and Marisol convinced her to host two farm dinners at her house every week so that we could all get in to cook and clean a bit. We left plenty of leftovers."

"That's lovely," Ava said. "Thank you."

Greta shrugged, and the corners of her mouth twitched downwards. "It wasn't enough."

Marisol patted the young woman's back in passing and said something that Ava didn't understand. She gave Lucia a questioning look, and the girl translated, "Mami says that sometimes *viejas* get sick, and it's nobody's fault." The little girl crossed her arms and stuck out her lower lip in a pout. "But it is. It's Gran's fault. If she had let Mami help her, she wouldn't have had to go to the hospital. Mami can fix anything." Lucia scrubbed at a clean bit of tile in a half-hearted way and then asked, "Do you think she just wanted to ride in an ambulance?"

Ava held back a smile and nodded at Lucia. "That could be part of it."

The girl sighed. She went to pull at her mother's shirt. "*Mami, tengo hambre.*"

"It's past lunch time, isn't it?" Ava said. She looked at Marisol and added, "I'm so grateful for your help today.

Would you join me at Gran's house for lunch? There's a big pot of lemon chicken soup on the stove."

"Yes, thanks," Marisol said with a smile. Greta nodded her agreement.

"You're welcome to go in and help yourself," Ava said. "I'll just wash out these buckets you brought and set them outside the back door to dry."

As the other women left, Ava looked around the old café kitchen with satisfaction. It still looked a bit empty and sad, but their efforts had brought the space one huge step closer to the bustling hub that Ava remembered. Marisol and Greta had helped her to do in a single day what would have taken her three, and Ava felt energized to tackle something else. Maybe after their late lunch, she would come back and start recipe testing.

A shadow darkened the back door, and Ava looked up, expecting one of the farm workers.

"The prodigal daughter returns," said a woman with the throaty voice of an old film star.

Ava knew that voice.

Her stomach flip-flopped as she stood to face her mother. "Hello, Lyra."

9

Beth

BETH WAS SO busy learning the inner workings of Imagine Knit and settling into her new home upstairs that she had hardly a moment to spare for thinking about Josh. He had texted her twice, wanting to know how she was holding up, and she had sent perfunctory responses. Seeing him on the day that she returned his apartment keys and picked up the last of her stuff had hurt like hell, but it seemed as if she had left her love for Josh back in Maine and her bitter disappointment behind in Half Moon Bay.

Redwood Grove was her fresh start. The true beginning of her life as an adult. And though she hadn't been here long, Beth was loving every moment. She adored the steely, shockingly generous woman who had hired her. Yolanda deserved a truly spectacular Christmas present, and Beth was already poring over designs, trying to decide what sort of sweater or shawl she wanted to knit for the woman who had saved her from slinking back to Maine in defeat.

Beth loved learning the ins and outs of Imagine Knit's inventory and discussing potential projects with customers. She loved filling her little old fridge with phenomenal local produce and throwing together easy, delicious meals for one. And most of all, she loved exploring her new town and the surrounding redwoods in the golden hours after the shop closed.

The bell tinkled over the front door of the shop, and so Beth set her knitting aside and snapped to attention. The customer looked even younger than Beth, maybe still in high school, though her heavy makeup and oversized army jacket made it hard to tell exactly how old she was.

"Good morning," Beth greeted her brightly. The girl smiled and nodded in silent greeting before ducking behind a shelf packed with richly dyed merino wool. Beth gave her a minute to browse and then asked, "Are you looking for anything in particular?"

The girl shrugged and said in a low voice, "I haven't made anything in a while."

"Do you knit or crochet?"

"Knit. My mom taught me years ago."

"That's cool," Beth said brightly. "I'm the only knitter in my family. It must be fun to have someone in the house who knows what she's doing."

"She wasn't very good," the girl said quietly. "And she's not around right now."

"Oh." Beth paused, feeling foolish. "I'm sorry to hear that."

The girl gave her a sad smile and drifted a bit closer,

running her hands over soft skeins of lambs' wool as she moved down the aisle.

"My name is Beth. What's yours?"

"Juniper."

"It's nice to meet you, Juniper. I don't meet many knitters close to my own age."

"I thought it would be nice to make a hat for my aunt," Juniper said, picking up a lovely skein of fir-green yarn. "I'm staying with her for a while. My mom's in rehab. Again."

Beth's heart broke for her, but she made sure there was no pity in her voice when she replied. "That must be hard. My mom was always there for me, but I know what it's like to have a parent who, well, wasn't. I guess my dad was pretty messed up. I never really knew him. He's gone now."

"That's probably for the best," Juniper said in a voice that seemed to be on the verge of tears. "Not knowing him, I mean. It's harder when you do." She looked up at Beth with a watery smile and said, "My mom's pretty great when she's clean. We have fun. But it never lasts long."

Beth nodded. She had no idea what to say, but she could at least listen.

"She's the one who taught me to knit," Juniper went on. "She learned in one of the fancy rehab places that my grandpa sent her to before he cut her off. She got really into it for a while, and she would teach me what she'd learned each week when my dad took me to see her."

Juniper was quiet for a while, looking down at the yarn in her hands. Slowly, she reached into the bargain bin and pulled out a skein of turquoise blue yarn.

"Maybe I'll make a hat for her too." She looked up at Beth with a crooked smile and said, "I'm not sure I remember how.

I mean, I remember how to knit, but I don't really remember how to, um, get the yarn on the needles to start with. Casting on, is that what it's called?"

"Yep!" Beth grinned. "I can help with that. I still can't believe I get paid to talk about knitting!"

Juniper laughed. It was a cheerful sound, if still kind of shaky. She walked up to the counter.

"Have you heard of Ravelry?" Beth asked.

"No," Juniper said. "What's that?"

"It's a website full of knitting patterns. Lots of them are free. We'll find something you like and I can help you cast on. If you run into trouble, you're welcome to come back for help. Or you can always get on YouTube and look up any techniques that you don't know how to do. That's how I taught myself to knit. All YouTube videos."

"You taught yourself? That's impressive."

Beth laughed and shook her head. "No, it's easy. You'll see." She pulled up the website and clicked over to the first page of free hat patterns. Juniper's eyes widened, and she stepped closer to the screen.

"Do you think I could do that?" she asked, pointing to a cap with a simple cable design.

"Definitely!" Beth looked at the yarns that Juniper had chosen and said, "Let's see... you'll probably need five millimeter needles for these. A sixteen-inch circular needle would work best. We have metal or bamboo."

"I think I've just used plastic and wooden needles," Juniper said, looking uncertainly at the wall of knitting needles and other accouterments that hung behind Beth. "Which do you like better?"

"Well, I use metal now because they're faster. But I

remember I hated them when I was getting started, because they're so smooth that your work can slip right off if you're not careful. So for your first cable-knit hats, I'd go with the bamboo."

"Bamboo it is. Could I, I mean—" Juniper stuttered to a stop and tried again. "Do you have time to show me how to knit cables?"

"I'm pretty busy with all these other customers," Beth joked as she gestured around the empty store. Juniper raised an eyebrow, and Beth laughed. "I would love to help you. Grab that stool over there while I ring you up, and then you can sit behind the counter with me."

Once Juniper was seated beside her, Beth showed her how to cast on. "The first few rounds are easy, see? Just knit and purl. You do that while I dust and sweep, and then I'll show you how to use a cable needle."

By lunchtime, Juniper's first hat was off to a flying start. She talked about her struggles with school – the academics were easy enough for Juniper; it was everything else that felt like a struggle to her – and the temporary sanctuary she had found in her aunt's incredible gardens. In turn, Beth told her about Cherry Blossom Point and the long-lost aunt who had come into their lives when Beth was already in her first year of college. Just a few hours into their acquaintanceship, they felt like fast friends.

"Do you get a lunch break?" Juniper asked as she put her half-finished hat into her backpack.

"Yep," Beth said. "There's a little back-in-thirty sign for me to put in the front window. Not that anyone's likely to stop by... I'm not sure how this place is still open, if one single customer is a normal morning."

"It's just a weekday," Juniper said. "Redwood Grove gets busy on weekends. People come up from Santa Cruz, or even San Jose and San Francisco. Especially in the summertime. There's a huge campground at the state park down the road, and all the campers love to come into town to eat and shop."

"You sound like a local," Beth told her as they walked outside.

"I am," Juniper said lightly. "I was born here. In a yurt in the woods, if you can believe it. We didn't move down to Santa Cruz until I was ten. My mom had been good for a few years..." Juniper trailed off and shook her head. "Anyway. Let me buy you lunch."

"Oh, no. I couldn't."

"Please? Do you know how much most people would charge for the sort of three-hour lesson you just gave me? Lunch is the least I can do. We can just get something from the hot bar at the grocery store. They have amazing chili verde. And we can eat on those tables in the sunshine there."

"Okay," Beth relented. She put the lunch sign on the door and locked the shop up tight. "But next time, it's my treat."

"You're a really good teacher, you know," Juniper said as they crossed the street. "You should teach classes. You'd be making your own customers."

"That's a good idea," Beth said. "I'll have to talk to Yolanda about it. She's gone all day today. Her son drove her to visit a friend at the hospital in San Jose."

"That must be Gran," Juniper said. "They're old friends. I need to get over there." She bumped Beth's hip with her own and smiled. "You'll have to come meet her as soon as she's home. It might be strawberry season by then, and she's got a whole farm full of them. You'll love it."

"It's a plan," Beth agreed. She linked her elbow with Juniper's, and they walked into the grocery store arm in arm.

It seemed as though Beth was putting down roots in Redwood Grove.

So what if she didn't stay forever?

Right now, she was exactly where she needed to be.

10

Ava

Ava felt a strange sense of dissociation standing out on the back porch of the café with her mother. Lyra was dressed in fitted jeans and a flowing shirt, her brand-new cowboy boots just slightly dusted by their walk from the white convertible she had somehow maneuvered up the dirt road. Her golden hair was protected from the spring sunshine by a silk scarf that picked up the accent colors in her blouse.

Lyra was sixty and still breathtakingly beautiful. But as ever, her beauty was the untouchable kind. Aside from holding hands in a crowd or the occasional awkward hug, Ava had no memories of her mother touching her as a child. No caresses, no cuddles. Being next to her now brought up the usual storm of emotions: grief and anger all tied up in a squashed and desperate desire to be loved.

"How long have you been here?" Lyra asked, lifting her

oversized sunglasses from her eyes to her hairline. "You didn't tell me that you were coming."

"I tried to call you when I heard about Gran," Ava said tiredly.

Greta peeked out of Gran's front door.

Ava waved to her and called, "You go ahead and eat! I'll be there in a few."

What little appetite Ava had worked up cleaning the café had deserted her.

"I never got a call from you," Lyra said.

"Your number was disconnected," Ava said. "I just got an error message."

"Oh, *that* old number? I've had my new one for... gosh, nearly two years now!"

Ava nodded. That sounded about right. "So how did you find out?"

"Patricia Flores heard the news through the grapevine and messaged me on Facebook. You can always find me there, you know."

The orange farm cat rubbed the side of his face against Ava's leg, and she crouched down to pet him. She wasn't surprised that Toni's stepmother had found a way to gossip with even the far-flung natives of Redwood Grove. What surprised her was the fact that her mother had actually *come.*

"Where are you living now?" Ava asked.

"Really, Avalon," Lyra huffed with exasperation. "I am *living* in the same place I have been living for *years.*"

It took a moment for Ava to wrack her brain for her mother's last-known place of residence. "Palm Springs?"

"*Yes*, Palm Springs. For goodness sake... Richard and I are quite happy there."

That was nearly three years with the same man in the same place. Quite possibly a record for Lyra Hoffman. It also meant that Lyra had lived...what? Two hours and twenty minutes away from her daughter's San Diego home? For the past three years. And she hadn't visited once.

Then again, neither had Ava.

"Have you been to see Gran yet?" Ava asked.

"You know how I hate hospitals," Lyra said with a toss of her hair.

"Gran hates hospitals. And she's stuck in one."

Lyra looked away. "Well, I'm not."

Ava looked at her in disbelief. "So why are you here?"

"Oh, I'll go see her," Lyra said dismissively. "I just wasn't up for it after such a long drive. I need a good night's sleep before I get back behind the wheel."

"You're staying here?"

"Well, where *else* would I stay, Avalon? Really."

Ava swallowed and nodded. "Okay. Do you want some soup? We were about to sit down for lunch."

"A light lunch sounds lovely." Lyra tripped lightly down the stairs, and Ava admired her mother's grace and energy. She hoped that she was still that healthy twenty years from now. Gran had been the same, Ava remembered as she followed her mother into the house. She hadn't slowed down one iota when she hit sixty. And her strength had waned so gradually afterwards that Ava had hardly noticed, had still thought of her grandmother as being as full of vim and vigor as ever.

"That smells wonderful!" Lyra exclaimed as they walked into the kitchen. The aroma of the soup that had been simmering all day filled the air with savor and citrus and fresh cilantro that one of the other women had added at the last minute. "Be a dear and serve me a bowl, would you? Is there lemonade?"

Greta dutifully ladled out a bowl of lemon chicken soup as Marisol gave Ava a questioning look.

"This is my mother, Lyra."

"We'll keep this place shipshape until Gran gets home," Lyra told her. Greta set a bowl of soup in front of her, and Lyra flashed her a smile. "Thank you, dear."

Ava had no appetite, but she forced herself to join the other women at the table and eat a bowl of chicken soup. It was delicious, rich and lemony, and her nerves settled somewhat as her stomach filled. Any awkward gaps in the conversation were filled by Lucia, who was happy to chatter on about school and strawberry season and her friend's purple dress. After Marisol and Lucia went home, when Greta was washing dishes and Lyra had gone to freshen up, Ava slipped outside.

There was a pale blue bicycle leaning against the back of the café, an ancient cruiser that Ava had ridden as a teenager. Someone must have been taking care of it, because it moved perfectly smoothly as she rolled it out into the sunshine. She hopped onto her old bike and coasted down the road.

As agitated as Ava felt, the sunlight and movement worked their magic quickly. There was a sense of freedom that overtook her as she flew down the familiar road. She left all of the complicated feelings that her mother triggered behind her, in the cloud of dust that rose from the dirt.

Ava had been so busy visiting the hospital and working on Gran's house and the café that she hadn't taken any time to explore the farm itself. Coasting down the back road, she realized that she hadn't explored the farm in quite some time. She came to visit Gran fairly frequently, but she rarely strayed beyond the main house anymore. When Ava did visit, she wanted to soak up every moment of her time with her grandmother. She never wandered through the fields the way she had as a little girl.

As a small child, this farm had been her entire world. Some of her earliest and most vivid memories were of the long lines of the strawberry fields, chatting with the workers in Spanglish and making a lunch of the sun-warmed berries as she sat in the dirt under the blue sky.

Seeing them now was strange. When she was a little girl, the fields had seemed endless, stretching from one horizon to the next. It hit her now how small the farm actually was, just a few hectares of coveted land that stretched from the highway to the mountain foothills beyond. It was no wonder that Gran's finances were in such a state. As Ava neared the back boundary of the property, she saw the diversified fields that Nolan had started a few years before. In an effort to bring more year-round income to the farm, they now grew an assortment of herbs and vegetables in addition to the strawberries that fruited in early summer. From the road, Ava could see Brussels sprouts and carrots and broad-leafed root vegetables that she couldn't identify.

There was a figure working in the field, and as Ava got closer, she recognized Nolan's wavy auburn hair beneath a sun-bleached baseball cap. She coasted to a stop nearby as he straightened up at the edge of the field. He had filled a huge box with softball-sized root vegetables that Ava didn't recognize.

"What are those?" she asked.

Nolan looked up with a start; when his eyes landed on Ava, a smile spread slowly across his face. After a moment he replied, "Watermelon radishes. They grow as quickly as any other radishes, but they sell for about three times as much. They're one of our best sellers at the market this time of year."

He took a knife out of his pocket, unfolded it, and cut a segment out of one of the globes. The watermelon radishes ranged from pale cream to sage green on the outside, but inside, they were a vibrant shade of pink. Ava accepted the segment and bit into it. It was cool and bitter, a bit spicy, and she couldn't help but laugh at her own surprise.

"It just tastes like a regular radish."

Nolan grinned. "People pay a premium for the color, though."

"I shouldn't be surprised."

"We've been looking into other varieties as well," Nolan told her. "Gran trials new varieties in her garden, and then we take the ones that thrive in this microclimate and put a larger order in the next year for our market garden."

Nolan walked through the field to where the watermelon radishes gave way to something smaller and plucked a small purple radish from the ground. He cut it open to reveal a bright amethyst interior.

"We've got every color of radish at this point," he said. "There are even lime green ones available these days. We have white, black, yellow, pink. And yes," he added with a twinkle of good-natured teasing in his eyes, "they all taste like radishes. But people keep buying them. They stand out, and market shoppers love their rainbow salads."

"What else do you grow?" Ava asked. "I saw Brussels

sprouts, and of course there are always strawberries, but what else?"

"We've been growing more and more herbs the past few years," Nolan said.

"Medicinal herbs?"

"No, I wouldn't know where to start with those," Nolan replied. "But people pay a premium for fresh culinary herbs. We've dedicated a full acre this year to thyme, cilantro, fennel, dill... all kinds of things. And of course we have our perennials, like rosemary and sage. In the spring and fall, when there are no strawberries to bring to market, the herbs make up nearly half of our sales. And they don't take up nearly as much room in the truck as watermelon radishes."

Ava felt a rush of warmth for this man who tended so carefully to her grandmother's land.

"I can't tell you what a comfort it is to me to have you holding down the farm while Gran is ill," Ava told him. "But if this farm is going to pay for the level of care that Gran is going to need this coming year, we need to do more."

"Marisol told me about your plans for the café."

"News travels fast around here," Ava said with strained levity. Was there something between Nolan and the beautiful single mother who lived on the farm? Ava pushed aside a flare of jealousy. So what if there was? Marisol was lovely.

"It's a small world, and the farm is smaller," Nolan said. "I think that the farm café is a great idea, if you can find the right people to run it."

"It's a start," Ava said, "but I don't know if it will be enough."

They were quiet for a moment, looking out over the field. Then Ava said, "My mother showed up today."

"Good ol' Lyra," Nolan said. His voice was dead serious – but a moment later, he gave her a mischievous grin. "And you ran away?"

"I did," Ava said with a nervous laugh. "Is that horrible?"

"Were you expecting her?" he asked quietly.

"I haven't spoken to her in years," Ava admitted. She sighed. "I suppose that I should leave the past in the past and just move forward, but I am not sure how to do that. Not with her."

"It's easier said than done, that's for sure." Nolan looked at her thoughtfully, and his teal eyes made Ava so nervous that she looked away without really wanting to.

"I should be getting back."

"I don't know how long your mother is staying," Nolan said quickly as Ava got back on her bike. "And I know that you have a million other things that you need to do, but if you want to get away..." he paused for just a moment and continued, "come find me. We could get off the farm and down to the beach for a bit, for you to catch your breath. I would say tomorrow morning, but Saturday is our biggest market day. And Jose is out sick, so it's just me."

"Can I come?" Ava asked without thinking. God, what was wrong with her? She didn't even know this man. But the teenage girl in her was still head over heels with the boy he used to be, and sometimes she just... forgot herself.

Being with him, being together, that ship had sailed a long time ago. But he loved Gran, and he loved this farm. They were together on that. And that comforted Ava as much as it frightened her. "I would love to help."

Nolan grinned. "I'd like that. I leave at four-thirty. Still want to come?"

"I've been gone a long time," Ava said, "but I do remember how markets work. I ran most of the stands myself when I was seventeen."

"I remember," Nolan said softly.

Ava took a step back and put a hand on her bike. "I'll see you tomorrow morning."

Nolan gave her a smile that made her heart do an utterly unprofessional somersault. "I'm looking forward to it."

11

Toni

"Getting up before the sun is sacrilege," Juniper muttered as they loaded Toni's truck.

"Which religion are we sacking?" Toni asked.

"I worship both the sun and sleep," Juniper told her with exaggerated stodginess. "Waking up before the crack of dawn is an insult to both of the things I hold so dear to my heart."

"Hop in the truck. There's tea waiting in the cupholder."

Juniper peered at her in the dim glow of the porch light. "Is it caffeinated?"

"It's four-thirty in the morning," Toni told her niece. "Of *course* it's caffeinated."

"Excellent." Swishing the blanket around her shoulders like a queen's cloak, Juniper swanned off to the passenger-side door.

Toni shook her head and chuckled as she hefted the last

box of farmers-market wares into her truck and made sure everything was tucked in tightly. She *liked* having her oldest niece around. Let people say what they wanted about kids these days; this particular teenager was one of Toni's favorite human beings on the planet. She always had been, and Toni was in no hurry to return her to her father.

Ethan had called her back and left a message, but they hadn't actually spoken. They had missed each other's calls a few times and then reverted to text messages. Ethan had agreed to let Juniper stay through the weekend, so long as she was back in school on Monday morning. Even in the voice message that he had left, Toni could hear her younger brother's exhaustion. What must it feel like to drop the love of his life off at rehab for the umpteenth time? To be left to care for their teenage daughter all on his own? Juniper hadn't outright said anything against her dad, but she had hinted that they hadn't been getting along so well for a while now. But in Toni's eyes, she was just as delightful at sixteen as she had been at any other age... maybe even more so now that she could be trusted not to rip up Toni's books or bring her glass jars of herbal oils crashing down from their shelves.

Then again, she wasn't Juniper's parent, and she'd never tried to exert any real control over the niece who, in her eyes, was almost grown. That made for an easy friendship. Ethan, it seemed, still saw a little girl when he looked at his tall, spiky-haired daughter. And he still treated her like one, which Juniper was growing to resent.

"Ready?" Toni asked as she climbed up into the leather seat of her trusty old truck.

Juniper let out a cartoon-like snore in response, head lolling back dramatically. Toni just laughed and started the ignition. Her niece liked to complain, but Toni hadn't asked Juniper to help her with the farmers market. Juniper had volunteered, knowing full well what time Toni left on Saturday mornings. And Juniper had done most of the work of loading the truck herself.

They were quiet on the long drive south, listening to a Golden Oldies station and watching the sky over the ocean shift slowly from black to gray. Juniper's knitting needles stayed in motion the whole time, working around and around the circle of a hat in progress. When they reached the Aptos farmers market, Juniper hopped to work straight away, and they had the tent and displays set up in record time. In addition to fresh herbs and flowers, Toni sold loose-leaf herbal teas, tinctures, salves, and herbal body oils. Between the bouquets and her many-colored labels, Toni's stand was the most inviting one at the market. She'd come a long way from her first market nearly a decade before, where she had set up a single table with bundles of sage and wildflower bouquets.

"Looks like the coffee stand is up and running," Juniper said as Toni straightened her large banner sign that read *Antonia's Biodynamic Herbs.* "Can I get you something?"

"I'll take one of their lavender lattes," Toni requested. "Thank you."

Juniper skipped off down the row, no worse for wear after their predawn drive. Toni gave her stand a once-over and checked her watch. Usually she was still setting things out when market-goers started trickling in around eight, but with Juniper's help, the stand was ready a full half hour early. Toni smiled and sauntered in the direction of the stall that sold her favorite baked goods. She did a double-take as she passed Hoffman Farm's two-tent setup.

"Avalon?" she exclaimed, surprised into using her best friend's full first name. "I didn't expect to see you here!"

"Hi, Toni!" Ava set down the box of spring produce she was carrying and hurried out to give Toni a hug. "I wasn't planning on it, but I ended up filling in last minute."

Toni glanced over her friend's shoulder at Gran's handsome farm manager and gave Ava a knowing look. "Did you now?"

Ava blushed, suddenly looking very much like the adolescent girl Toni remembered so fondly. "Stop that. I'm only here for Gran."

"Sure," Toni said, drawing the word out. "Keeping it professional."

Ava looked over her shoulder to make sure Nolan was nowhere near them, and Toni cackled. Ava looked back at her and gave her a light shove. "Go away, Toni."

"Gladly. Have fun."

"So nice seeing you," Ava said, pushing Toni in the direction she had been walking when she passed by. "I'd love to talk, but I have radishes to unload. Bye bye now!"

Toni chuckled and trotted off down the row to buy a couple of scones for her and Juniper. When she walked by the Hoffman Farmstand again, she couldn't help but note how beautiful Ava looked. She was dressed in a plaid shirt and jeans with no makeup, but she looked more alive than Toni had seen her in... well, too long. Her hair was up in a messy bun, golden strands falling here and there around her face. The crisp morning air had turned her cheeks a girlish shade of pink, and her sky-blue eyes were bright. It was no wonder Nolan could hardly keep his eyes off of her.

Toni walked on with a spring in her step, suddenly hopeful that she would be seeing a whole lot more of her dearest friend. It was about time, too. San Diego's loss was her gain.

"There you are!" Juniper exclaimed when she spotted her. "You left the stand unattended!"

"Did you have to chase away tincture-stealing bandits?" Toni asked.

Juniper nodded solemnly. "Hordes. They nearly made off with your lupine bouquets."

"Well," Toni said, matching her niece's solemn absurdity, "I am deeply grateful that you were able to prevent that travesty. I offer scones as tribute."

Juniper snatched at the bag and peeked into it, playacting forgotten. "What kind are they?"

"One's a lemon scone with citrus sugar. The other one is honey-walnut."

"Yum!" Juniper said, plucking the sugary scone from the bag. "Citrus, please!"

"Very well." Toni bowed to her niece before taking the remaining scone, and Juniper giggled. They sat shoulder to shoulder on Toni's small folding bench as they ate, watching the farmers market piece itself together beneath a pearl-gray sky.

"Do you think that people will come out in this?" Juniper asked after a while.

"It'll burn off by mid-morning," Toni replied. "And you'd be surprised. We even get a decent turnout on rainy days. Wait and see."

The market was as busy as usual, but to Toni, it felt like a leisurely day. Juniper handled each and every transaction, leaving Toni free to pour out samples of her Bed-Thyme Chamomile Tea and chat about biodynamic farming with curious customers. Now and then, Ava's laughter filtered through the crowd, and the sound of it lifted Toni's heart. It was good to see her best friend looking more like herself again.

Even before Gran had landed herself in the hospital, Ava had been living as a shadow of the vibrant young woman that Toni remembered. From what Toni had seen of Ava's nearly twenty-year marriage, the relationship had bordered on abusive. And yet even after it ended, Ava never seemed to break free of it. She just kept spinning her wheels, working that same old job to pay the rent in a city that she didn't truly love.

Maybe Gran's close call was the slap upside the head that Ava had needed.

Toni sure hoped so.

With Juniper's help, Toni made nearly twice as many sales as she usually did on gloomy spring mornings. They went through three large teapots of samples and completely sold out of fresh flowers, with the exception of a special bouquet Toni had set aside. And together, they were able to pack everything up after the market in half the time.

"What would you say to driving over the hill before we head home?" Toni asked as they closed up the back of her truck. "To see Gran?"

"I haven't seen her in ages," Juniper said immediately. "I'd love to go visit."

Toni grinned and tousled her niece's hair. Free of product

this morning, it had plenty of body and personality all on its own. Juniper's hair had been straight as a little girl, but it had gotten progressively wavier over the past few years. Not the crazy mass of curls that Toni had, but the perfect waves that most women longed for. And Juniper had left them on the cutting room floor. Well, if a bad haircut and a few too many piercings were the worst decisions that she made at sixteen, she was doing a hell of a lot better than Toni.

"That was a pretty good market, huh?" Juniper asked as they pulled onto the highway.

"The best I've had so far this year," Toni agreed. "By a mile."

"Can I help you every week?"

"I would love that! I can pick you up on my way through Santa Cruz."

Juniper was quiet for a while, and Toni realized that wasn't the response her niece had been hoping for. Toni waited a while, but Juniper didn't offer any insight into her worries. She just stared out the window, looking forlorn.

"What's up, Junebug?"

"I don't know, Nia." Juniper gave her a sad little smile. "I guess I was hoping I could help you with everything. The garden, the tinctures and teas... I would love to learn all that."

"What about school?"

"I hate it," Juniper said softly.

"How can you hate school?" Toni asked. "You're brilliant."

"I love learning. But school's not about that. Not really. I have to read the things *they* want me to read and come up with the answers that they want to hear. Anyway, this year is basically done. All the AP tests were last week, so I'm done with Statistics and History and Bio and Psych. We're still supposed to go to those classes every day, but we're just killing time. And I already wrote the final English essay that's due next month. There's no way out of P.E., but come *on*, Nia. Why should I have to run in circles on a plastic track instead of surfing or hiking through the redwoods? I hate it. I would learn so much more working with you."

"I would love that, Junebug, but it's not up to me. What will your dad say?"

Juniper was quiet for a long moment. "He'll come around."

"What about your friends?" Toni asked. The question earned her another long silence, and they were halfway to San Jose before Juniper spoke again.

"They're all into drugs now," she said at last, her voice hardly audible over the hum of the highway. "Every weekend. After school. Even between classes sometimes."

"But... you hang out with the smart kids."

Juniper made a derisive little sound. "Yep. That's Santa Cruz. Even the straight-A students who are holding down part-time jobs are popping pills on the weekends. Hell, most of them take pills on weekdays, too, just a different kind. I can't walk to school in the morning without walking through clouds of smoke."

"And are they pressuring you to try those things too?"

"No, not really. My friends are cool about it. They know about my mom, and how I feel about it all... but that doesn't stop *them* from doing that stuff. It's all they do when they hang out anymore. And I just feel so... outside of things."

"That sounds hard," Toni murmured.

"I'm so scared, Nia." In that moment, Juniper sounded

like the little girl Toni remembered. "I'm scared for them, and I'm scared for me."

Toni reached over and took Juniper's hand. She understood the girl's fears. Toni had watched Ethan's pretty girlfriend waste away into a hollow shell of a woman, bit by bit. Juniper's mother had tried. She had stayed clean all through her pregnancy and for long stretches of time throughout Juniper's childhood... but each hopeful recovery had ended in heartbreak.

"I can't believe that all the top students are... I mean, I believe *you*," Toni said. "But man. I thought your generation was smarter than mine."

"Maybe in some places they are," Juniper murmured. "My friends *think* they are. They think they're too smart to get hooked on any of it."

"If they're partying like that every weekend, it sounds like they're already hooked."

Juniper nodded, looking glum, and they were both quiet as Toni took the exit toward the hospital. She found a shady spot on the edge of the hospital parking lot and led her niece into the building. Juniper carried the fresh bouquet that Toni had set aside for Gran, and Toni carried two thermoses: one with bone-knit tea and another with cream of asparagus soup. They went up to Gran's room in the intensive care unit, and Toni was shocked to see Gran's bed stripped and empty. She stood staring for a moment, then stumbled out into the hallway and flagged down the first nurse she could find, fearing the worst.

"We're looking for Margaret Hoffman."

"No need to look at me like I just killed your grandma." The nurse smiled and patted her arm. "Mrs. Hoffman is doing so well that she was transferred out of intensive care. She'll be here a good while yet, but she's out of the woods. I don't know which room she's in now, but you can go back down to the front desk and ask."

Toni blinked away tears of relief, only feeling the full force of her grief and fear when they started to recede. "Thank you."

They found Gran on the second floor, in a shared room with a dismal view of the parking lot. Her roommate was asleep and snoring like a freight train. When Toni saw Gran from the doorway, the woman looked as down as Toni had ever seen her. But the moment she caught sight of the two Flores girls, Gran's face brightened to her usual shine.

"Juniper! This *is* a surprise. I can't believe you came all the way to this dreadful city."

Juniper laughed lightly and hurried to Gran's bedside. "It's not all that far, Gran."

"These flowers are lovely. They're from Toni's garden, aren't they? There's no place like it. But sweetheart, what in the world have you done to your hair?"

"I cut it," Juniper told her, unfazed.

"Well, you're still beautiful." Gran's voice was just the slightest bit slurred, and Toni realized that the hospital must still have her on quite a high dose of pain meds. She glanced at Juniper, wondering if Gran's state might be triggering for a girl who had every reason to be extra sensitive about people in altered states, but the look that Juniper was giving Gran was one of pure adoration. Gran had that effect on people.

Toni smiled and walked to the cabinets in search of a vase. When she found one and set it by Gran's bedside, Juniper unbound the flowers and put them in one at a time.

"How are you, Antonia?" Gran brought the back of her hospital bed all the way up and took Toni's hand. "I know this isn't the first time you've come to visit me, but it's the first time that I feel awake and aware... more or less."

"I'm fine, Gran."

Her eyes narrowed. "Is that all I get? I lost my foot, child, not my mind."

Toni grinned and squeezed her hand. "Juniper helped me at the market today. It was wonderful."

"I'm moving back to Redwood Grove to be Nia's apprentice," Juniper said cheerfully.

Gran smiled. "Is that so?"

"It's a wonderful idea that's yet to be cleared with her legal guardian," Toni cut in.

Juniper stuck her tongue out at Toni. "I'll get emancipated."

Toni turned to Gran, her eyes widening in a silent plea for help. Gran just laughed. The old sci-fi noise of the *Doctor Who* theme song cut through the air, and Juniper checked her phone with a frown.

"It's my dad."

"Answer it."

Juniper rolled her eyes and raised the phone to her ear. "Hello, I love you, and I'm moving in with Nia."

"Oh craaaaap," Toni whispered.

"Buckle up, buttercup." Gran let out a guffaw, her natural good humor amplified by the pain meds. "I think we're in for a bumpy ride."

12

Ava

"Hey Mom!" Those two words – and Maggie's bright, beautiful voice – brought such a grin to Ava's face that the troubles of the past couple of weeks faded instantly to the background. She set down the kitchen knife that she was wielding and walked to the window, giving her daughter her full attention. "How's small-town living treating you?"

"It's a change of pace from San Diego, that's for sure," Ava said. "Honestly? I think I missed it."

"San Diego never really seemed to suit you. Kind of like... an oversized dinner jacket when you just want a comfy sweater."

"Very poetic," Ava said drily.

"I would never want to live there again. I love Portland, but city life is starting to wear on me. Toby and I have been talking about starting a homestead somewhere out in the boonies."

"How about these boonies?" Ava said.

Maggie made a sound like the air going out of a balloon. "Like we could afford land in coastal California. Get real, Mom. We're talking, like, Kentucky."

"Kentucky," Ava said flatly.

"I hear it's nice," Maggie said in the same tone. There was a beat of silence, and they both burst out laughing at the exact same time. "I don't know, Mom. Maybe we'll just travel for a while, work on organic farms, and study permaculture and stuff."

"I thought your business was going well?"

"Business is great," Maggie said. "We're booked solid through the spring, and that should be enough to keep us going through the winter when no one wants to hire garden planners."

"But that's when they need to be ordering seeds and working amendments into the soil."

"I try to tell 'em. Portlanders have short attention spans."

Ava snorted out a laugh. "So if business is booming, why leave?"

"I grow weary of this city life," Maggie said with high drama.

"I see," Ava said. She went back to the kitchen counter and put Maggie on speakerphone, picking up her knife again.

"It's nice enough in the summertime when people pay me to turn their pocket-sized lawns into gardens. But winters are rough. We've been talking about wintering somewhere sunny and doing the WWOOF thing–"

"*Woof?*" Ava interjected.

"Worldwide Workers on Organic Farms," Maggie said. "Remember? I wanted to do it years ago, but then Portland sucked me in like a black hole."

"You're really tired of that city, huh?"

"As cities go, it's not that bad." Maggie sounded like she was trying to convince herself of that. "But yeah, Mom. Tired of cities in general. It was fun when I was young–"

A sound escaped Ava that was partially a sputter of shock and mostly a laugh. "You *are* young. You're *so* young."

"But I'm tired of city life. The food is amazing, but I'd rather grow my own somewhere than pay through the nose for it here."

"You and Toby are always welcome here," Ava said.

"I know, Mom. Thank you. I miss you and Gran so much, you have no idea. But we really are busy right now. I might be able to make it down for a quick visit soon, but Toby would have to hold down the fort here with our two-person business. We have consultations literally every day. And the planning stuff I can do remotely, but we're out tilling and getting the ground ready every day, and it will be time to plant soon. Not to mention all of our little greenhouse babies."

"No pressure, Maggie."

"I know, Mom. Thanks. But enough about me."

"I could never hear enough about you."

"How's Auntie Lyra?" Maggie teased. She was too young to remember her then-forty-year-old grandmother requesting to be called Auntie instead of Gran, but Ava had mentioned it at some point, and Maggie had found it absolutely hilarious. It hadn't seemed so funny at the time.

"She's fine," Ava said.

"That's all I get?"

Ava leaned closer to the phone and said in an undertone, "She's *in* the building."

Ava's mother rarely emerged from her room – and Lyra had enough phone conversations in there for Ava to know that the walls were mostly soundproof – but she just couldn't start a conversation about her mother knowing that Lyra might walk out at any moment.

"Fine, fine. But I'm calling back later for all the deets."

"The deets, huh?"

"Yes, mother dearest. Drama in full detail."

"There hasn't been any drama," Ava said, unable to keep the surprise from her voice.

"Well, that doesn't sound like you and dear Auntie Lyra," Maggie said.

"You hush. She's been..." Ava paused and peered around the corner to reassure herself that she was the only one downstairs. "She's been surprisingly helpful. Mostly she's been keeping to herself, but she helped me to make sense of Gran's books and get all the employees paid on time."

"Doesn't Gran have a farm manager for that?"

Ava swallowed and said, "He manages the fields and sales, but it seems like Gran still had a tight grip on the rest of the finances."

Maggie made a noncommittal sound. "And the café?"

"Coming along. It's clean, and I've ordered everything we'll need for the grand reopening." She had sunk most of her savings into the place, in fact. But that wasn't something that she needed to mention to her daughter – or anyone else, for that matter. She wasn't paying rent at the moment, so it wasn't as if she was in dire financial straits. Her retirement fund was safely growing with the market, more or less doubling each decade, and Ava had no intentions of touching *that* for another twenty years or more. She could afford to invest a bit of money in this place that had invested so much in her.

"I'm going to do everything I can to make it down for that," Maggie said. "I'll work overtime on all the garden plans in the meantime, and Toby can handle the execution without me for a bit."

"I would love that." Ava dumped the last of the veggies into the soup pot and left them to simmer. "Hey, have you heard from your brother?"

"You haven't?" Maggie asked.

Ava was lucky if she could get a one-word reply to a text message. "Not lately."

"Yeah, we talked last weekend. He's good. Serious senior-itis, which I totally get."

"I don't suppose he's reconsidered applying to a few colleges? Keeping his options open?"

Maggie snorted. "College application deadlines are long gone, Mom."

"He could start at a community college," Ava protested weakly.

"That boy wants to be just like Dad. Don't be surprised if he enlists the *day* he turns eighteen."

Ava sighed. "He could have gone to college first and enlisted as an officer."

"That's not how Dad did it."

She let out another breath, very nearly regretting her marriage to a military man. Not that she could truly repent any decision that had given her two beautiful children. But she couldn't help the way that she felt – and when she pictured her son in uniform, she felt like crying. And not in a good way. They hadn't gotten enough time together, and now he was going to sign his life away and go off to God only knew what—

"Such sighs," Maggie teased, pulling Ava back to the present. "What's the weather like there?"

"Sunny," Ava admitted, looking out the kitchen window. Nolan was out there, refilling the dogs' water bowls.

"Get out and enjoy it."

"Thanks, sweetheart. I will."

"It was good talking to you, Mom. I love you."

"I love you too."

Ava set her phone down and wandered outside, where she sat down on the porch steps in the shade. Phoenix ran over and planted his head on her knee, trying to keep still even as his whole body wiggled with excitement. She laughed and scratched behind his ears while he stared up at her with adoration.

"How's it going?" Nolan asked.

Ava looked up at him with a start. She hadn't heard him walk across the yard; even his heavy boots were silent in the soft, dry dirt.

"It's going," she said. "I just posted a Help Wanted ad for the café to see if I can hire some people part time before the Grand Reopening."

"You look tired."

"Thanks," she said flatly, looking back down at Phoenix.

"I didn't mean—" Nolan trailed off and then tried again. "Is it 'head upstairs for a nap' kind of tired or 'in desperate need of an afternoon anywhere besides the farmhouse or the hospital' kind of tired?"

Ava let one side of her mouth quirk up in a reluctant smile. "The latter."

"I could use a break myself," Nolan said. "I was thinking about taking a quick drive up the One to clear my head. Do you want to come with me? Stop at a beach? You'll breathe easier."

Ava held his eyes for a long moment, unsure of what to make of his offer. A quick trip to a beach definitely sounded appealing... and so did the company. Hell, what did she have to lose? She had to go home sooner or later. What was the harm in spending a couple of hours with an old... friend?

"I haven't been to the beach since I got here," Ava admitted.

"That settles it," Nolan said. "Phoenix! Truck!"

Phoenix jumped up with a *woof* of joy and raced across the dirt access road to Nolan's truck, where he spun in circles in his excitement. Nolan caught up with him and opened up the back, and Phoenix jumped in.

Ava ducked into the house for a jacket – the beaches up the coast were overcast and windy more often than not – and a bottle of water. At the last moment, she gathered up some of the scones and muffins she had made in her flurry of recipe testing for the café. She wasn't a natural baker, but Gran's old family recipes had stood the test of time. When Ava followed them to the letter, everything came out delicious.

"Ready?" Nolan asked as she came back down the steps.

"Ready," she confirmed.

"I wasn't sure if you were going to come back out."

Nolan's voice was light, like he was joking, but there was a touch of nervousness there that touched her heart.

"I was gathering supplies." Ava reached into the paper bag that she held and pulled out a strawberry scone topped with lemon sugar. "Try this."

Nolan took a bite of the scone as he opened the passenger-side door with his spare hand. Ava climbed up into the truck and then turned and gave him an expectant look.

"Phenomenal," he assured her. "Just like Gran used to make."

"It's her mother's recipe."

"Priceless." Phoenix let out a whining yip in protest of their slow start, and Nolan chuckled. He closed Ava's door and circled around to join her inside of the cab.

They were quiet as he drove down the short dirt road and pulled onto Highway One. It was a gorgeous day on the central coast, bright and blustery without a hint of fog. The ocean shone a rare shade of turquoise blue, so different from the deep blue-gray of winter seas. Nolan drove at an easy pace, and they worked their way through the pastries that Ava had brought as they passed broad sand beaches where people flew kites and huddled against the wind-whipped sand.

They passed Pescadero State Beach, and Ava's heart gave a little flutter of recognition. Then Nolan pulled into an easy-to-miss parking area, just a little circle of road at the top of a cliff.

He parked and then turned toward her. "Feel like stretching your legs?"

"You remembered my favorite beach."

"Of course," Nolan said with a shrug. He'd always been

like that when they were young. Thoughtful. But he wasn't that boy anymore and hadn't been since he'd walked away, Ava reminded herself sternly as they climbed out of the truck and donned their windbreakers. No more than she was the fifteen-year-old girl who had fallen head over heels in love with him.

Phoenix pulled recklessly on his lead as Nolan tried to rein him in, and Ava followed them down the weathered wooden steps to the beach.

Ava met his eyes with a quick glance and looked back out over the water. "You remembered."

"Of course."

Pebble Beach had been Ava's favorite place to visit growing up. After Gran's farm, it might be her favorite place in the entire world. And yet somehow she had managed to go years without walking down these stairs.

A coastal breeze whipped past her, carrying a tang of salt, and Ava took a deep breath in. It was typical of this beach to be overcast and windy when every beach south of it was bathed in sunshine; this was where the San Francisco fog began most days. Ava didn't care. She loved it anyway. There was something holy about this place. Something perfectly zen.

At the bottom of the stairs, Nolan let Phoenix off his leash, and the dog took off down the beach at a joyous sprint. Nolan and Ava moved more slowly, picking their way across the rocks and down to the pebble beach. Beneath their feet, stretching all the way to the distant cliffs at the other end, were nothing but pebbles. Not a bit of sand, and no big rocks. Just tiny, polished stones roughly the size of her fingernails.

Ava crouched down and scooped up a handful of damp

pebbles from the waterline, bringing them up to examine them more closely. Clear white, bright red, dark green, gold... striped and spotted and bi-colored, each handful of pebbles was a feast for the eyes. A subdued rainbow underfoot, all the way down the beach. Ava kicked off her shoes and walked barefoot along the shoreline, enjoying the feeling of the cool pebbles shifting underfoot.

She loved to visit this beach as a teenager when she was in desperate need of a bit of peace. Sometimes she would even ride her bike all the way up the One just to sit on the beach and breathe. She could pass hours sifting through the pebbles in a meditative state, feeling the sun on her back and the wind on her face, listening to the endless rush of water against the rocky shore. The musical sound of waves on pebbles was like nothing else in the world, so different from the crash of waves against solid rock or sand. She wished that she could bottle it and take it home to San Diego to soothe her on those long, sleepless nights when she couldn't quiet her thoughts.

"Are you up for a bit of a hike?" Nolan asked.

She looked up at him in surprise. "Along the cliffs?"

"Where else?" he asked with a grin.

Ava shook her head, biting back a smile. "I'm too old to go mountain goating over boulders like we used to."

"I don't believe you."

The smile broke through, and Ava shook her head. "All right. I guess I could use a mini adventure."

"That's the spirit," Nolan said. They walked to the end of the beach, where the California coastline was crumbling into the sea in a series of rocks and boulders. Ava climbed an outcropping of rock and walked along the top of it. From there, it was just a hop, skip, and a jump to the next one. Picking her way along the smooth rocks was a breeze without shoes on, and it wasn't long before Ava got into the spirit of things. She and Nolan were nearly running along the coastline with Phoenix keeping pace down below.

After a while, the rocks gave way to another beach where pebbles mixed with sand. Ava jumped down a short distance, and her bare feet sank into the soft ground when she landed. She pulled them out with a laugh and then turned to Nolan, feeling his eyes on her.

"Too old for mountain goating," he said in a teasing voice. "I could hardly keep up with you."

"Maybe *you're* too old for mountain goating," she teased back.

"Never." He was quiet for a moment, teal-blue eyes holding hers. "You're glowing."

Ava brought a self-conscious hand to her cheek. She could feel the flush beneath her skin from the exercise and the fun of it, not to mention Nolan's eyes on hers. She turned away to look at the pearl-gray sky over the wind-whipped waves. "It's a glorious day. Thanks for getting me to the beach."

"Anytime," Nolan said.

Standing there with her feet in the sand and her eyes on the horizon, Ava felt whole. But her next thought was of her grandmother between four walls, and her heart sank. Nolan must have seen her expression shift, because he stepped closer with a look of concern on his face.

"What's wrong?"

Ava thought for a moment, wondering how to articulate her sudden grief. "It just hurts my heart to think of Gran stuck in a hospital bed while I'm out here enjoying the day."

"What's it going to take to bring her home?" Nolan asked.

Ava shrugged. "She's healing well so far, I think. When they discharge her from the hospital, they want to send her to some other long-term care facility. I haven't been to see it, but the pictures on their website looked dismal. And that's them putting their best face on. It must be even worse in person."

"Why can't she recover at the farm?"

"She still needs dressing changes, meds, physical therapy... I don't know what else. We can't afford in-home care, and I don't think that I would be able to take care of her well enough myself. Not yet, not while she's still healing from major surgery. The thought of sticking Gran in a home breaks my heart, but I don't know what else to do until she's fully healed."

Nolan gave her an odd look. "You know that Marisol's a nurse, right?"

Excitement coursed through Ava's body, and she turned away from the ocean to look him square in the face. "Marisol? Who lives on the farm?"

"Yes, that's the one," Nolan said with a quiet chuckle of amusement. "She's not certified in California yet, but she worked as a nurse in Mexico for a decade or more."

"And you think that she would agree to take care of Gran? We'd compensate her well, of course..."

"I know she would."

On impulse, Ava hugged him. Nolan wrapped his arms around her, and for just a moment, Ava's brain was clear of any coherent thought. His woodsy smell. His warmth and strength seeping into her... like a safe haven she so wanted to lean into.

She pulled away and forced a smile.

"Let's go talk to Marisol."

Nolan nodded. "Whatever you say, boss."

But there was a look in his eyes. Something that told her he'd felt it too. The past creeping in to remind them of how it used to be...

How it could be again.

She wheeled around and tromped through the sand back toward the truck. Because that whole train of thought was dangerous. The kind of thinking that could land her in a world of hurt.

She'd already been hurt by Nolan Pasternak once. She wasn't about to let it happen again.

13

Toni

WHEN TONI DROVE up her driveway, Ethan's car was already parked out front. A wave of exhaustion swamped her. She'd been up since four and had driven for nearly six hours on top of working the market. Dealing with her little brother was the last thing she wanted to do right now.

But whatever she was dealing with this week, Ethan had been dealing with worse. The love of his life was in rehab for the umpteenth time, and his teenage daughter was threatening to quit school and join her hippie aunt in the mountains.

Toni would need to be careful with how she dealt with this.

So when she went into her house to greet her uninvited guest, she did so with a smile.

"Ethan, when did you get here?"

"I've come to get my daughter," he growled. "She has school on Monday."

Ethan looked like he hadn't slept in days. There were bruise-like circles under his eyes, and his skin was tinted gray.

"Why don't you come inside?" Toni went into her house without waiting for a response.

"It's Saturday," Juniper griped as she kicked her shoes off at the door.

"We have church tomorrow," Ethan said.

"I don't *like* your weird hippie church."

"It's good for you."

"It's good for *you*. Gardening is good for me. And working the farmers market. It was your best day this year, right, Nia?"

"It was good to have a helper," Toni said. Ethan glared daggers at her, and she gave her little brother a level look. "I'll make some tea."

"I don't need *tea*, Toni. I need you to give this kid a kick in the butt and send her home to finish out the school year."

You go home, Toni wanted to tell him. *You have to take care of yourself before you can really be there for Juniper.* But she just pressed her lips tight and set about making tea. Nettles for a base, with some linden and mint. A bit of skullcap wouldn't go amiss today either...

As she started the tea brewing, Ethan and Juniper picked up their argument.

"I'm not going," Juniper said.

"You can't just leave a month before the school year ends. They'll fail you for that many absences, Juniper. It doesn't matter how high you score on the tests or how well written your essays are. They want butts in seats or they don't get funding."

"Dad, I hate it there." Juniper sounded close to tears.

"I never liked high school either, but I still graduated."

"I'm not dropping out!" Juniper shouted.

"That's right, you're not. Because you're going to class on Monday. End of story."

Juniper let out a sound of primal frustration. "You're not listening!"

"Hey, Junebug," Toni said softly as she carried the kettle through. "Could you give us a minute?"

"Good luck," Juniper spat as she stormed out.

The moment she was gone, Ethan put his head in his hands. "She has to come home, Toni."

"She needs more time." Toni put a gentle hand on her brother's shoulder. "So do you. Her school will understand. I can call and chat with her guidance counselor if you want me to."

Ethan's voice broke as he said, "I feel like I'm failing her."

Toni took a deep breath and patted her little brother on the back. "Juniper's an amazing kid. And you're a good dad. You're both struggling right now, that's all." She poured a cup of tea and added a heaping spoonful of honey.

"What if she never finishes high school?"

"You're catastrophizing, Ethan." Toni stirred the tea and handed it to him. He took it and stared down into the mug as if he didn't know what to do with it.

"The therapists say that she should stick to her usual routine," he muttered.

"Her normal routine isn't serving her," Toni said quietly. "Ethan, did you know that all of her friends are experimenting with drugs? That's a scary environment for any straight-edged kid, but for her in particular... she's terrified to go back."

Ethan's shoulders began to shake, and Toni realized that he was crying silently, tears falling down his cheeks and into his tea. Liquid sloshed over the side, and Ethan set the mug on Toni's coffee table with shaking hands.

"I don't know how to help her," he said brokenly, and Toni wondered if he meant Juniper or his wife.

"Let me take care of Juniper," Toni said. "You just take care of yourself for a while."

"What kind of man can't take care of his family?" Ethan asked, still not meeting her eyes.

One who's at the end of his rope.

"A man who's carried too much for too long," Toni said gently. "We're not far away. You can come visit whenever you'd like. Maybe even consider moving back to Redwood Grove for a while. You know Dad would be ecstatic." She picked up the tea and pressed it into his hands. "Everything will be okay. Juniper is an amazing kid."

"I know she is. I don't deserve her."

"Just let her be who she is, Ethan. Not every kid takes to school. Lord knows we didn't, and we turned out pretty okay, right? You should have seen her at the market today. She was amazing."

"Thanks, Toni. I guess she can stay here a few more days. I'll talk to her school."

Toni knew in her bones that Juniper needed more than

just a few days away from the dumpster fire of a home life her mother had saddled her with. But she wasn't going to push her brother any further. Not today.

"Focus on taking care of yourself for a while," she told him. "Juniper and I will get by just fine."

14

Ava

"Not today, Phoenix," Nolan said apologetically. He moved past the frantic golden retriever and went to open the gate, farm dogs at his heels.

"Here, dogs!" Ava called from the window of her car, trying to beckon them away from the back gate that opened onto a windy mountain road. They paid her no attention.

"Back, beasts!" Nolan shouted. Ava laughed in surprise as the dogs scattered and ran back toward the farm. Apparently *Back, beasts* was an established command. She would have to remember that one the next time she navigated one of the farm gates. For now, she simply drove through the gate and let Nolan latch it behind them before he climbed back into the passenger seat.

Despite her nerves at being alone with him again after their spontaneous hug that left her feeling irritatingly gushy inside, before they had even made it to the farm gate, his presence beside her felt... comfortable. Easy, even.

Maybe she could let things be easy. Yes, she and her grandmother's farm manager had a complicated history. But Ava didn't have to get tangled up in all of that. She could just let herself fall into the comfortable companionship of two people who had known each other as kids. Revive their old friendship without the distraction of teenage hormones.

Adults have hormones too, her brain reminded her helpfully.

"Sorry," Nolan murmured as his phone buzzed. He glanced at the screen and then gave Ava a questioning look. "It's a work call."

"Go ahead," she said, relieved for the interruption of her wayward thoughts. "Please."

"Jose," he answered in a tone that was both cheerful and brusque. "What's up?"

He listened for a moment and then responded, but most of it went over Ava's head. She picked up enough to make out that they were discussing an order to a local market that had gone awry, and Nolan said something about driving out there himself the next day.

"When did you learn to speak such fluent Spanish?" she asked when he hung up.

"Oh, that was in my early twenties," Nolan said. "When I started to pick it up, at least. That was in Baja, and then eventually on a farm in mainland Mexico. I felt like I lost all of my Spanish after that, but when I landed in Costa Rica in my thirties, it all came right back to me."

"That's when you were living on the same farm as Toni," Ava remembered.

"Our stays at Casa Tierra overlapped for a bit, yeah. I think she was there for about four years? And then she came back to California not long after I got there. I took over her job, actually. Until I got tired of life in the tropics and she landed me a job with Gran."

Ava pressed her teeth together to keep her jaw from dropping. *Toni* was the reason that Nolan had ended up at Hoffman Farm? Ava knew that the two of them had kept in touch – Toni had always been careful not to talk about Nolan to Ava, but she'd seen them together in group pictures on Facebook countless times over the years– but she'd had no idea that Toni and Gran had conspired to hire her high school sweetheart. All the way from Costa Rica, no less.

She let out a sigh. And this was exactly why. Because the very thought of it put her hackles up. The man was one of Toni's oldest and dearest friends, and Gran had nestled him right under her wing with the rest of them during the years that Nolan and Ava and Toni were inseparable.

Why did Ava care so much, so many years after a teenage heartbreak? Every time she thought that she was over the man, something would happen to show her just how deluded she was. She would see a picture of him on social media or Gran would mention his name, and it would all come rushing back to her. All that love and heartbreak that had carved out a permanent home for itself in her heart. There were times that she *had* successfully forgotten about him for months on end... and then out of nowhere he invaded her dreams, and she would wake up flooded with old memories... or just an impression of Nolan's smiling face and a feeling of pure joy at being in his presence again. And that feeling would haunt her for days because it outshone anything that she felt in her daily life.

"Thinking about Gran?" Nolan guessed. His tone was full of compassionate understanding. Ava just nodded, wanting to agree but not quite able to give voice to a lie. She *should* be thinking about Gran. What was wrong with her?

"Marisol's with her," he said. "She said she'd go straight over after dropping Lucia at school."

"She's a godsend," Ava murmured. "What's a nurse doing working on Gran's farm?"

"Her parents passed away a few years back," Nolan said, "and they were the only family she had left in Mexico. Her brothers both live in Half Moon Bay, and they have cousins scattered all over the place. She wanted Lucia to grow up close to family, so she moved here... about nine months ago? At the beginning of the school year. Jose's her cousin, so he secured her a Hoffman cabin that was empty. She wanted to be close to family but not actually live with them."

"And she works on the farm?"

"Yep. More hours some seasons than others, but it evens out."

They were quiet for a while, listening to old country songs on the radio until the station started to fizz and crackle. Nolan switched it off, and Ava could feel his eyes on her face. She stared stubbornly ahead, eyes on the mountain road.

"What about you?" Nolan asked softly. "How's life in San Diego?"

"Quiet," Ava admitted. "Maggie moved out years ago, and Ryan's a high school senior who's gone more often than he's home. They were my whole life for so long that lately my life feels pretty empty." She pressed her lips together then, surprised by her own honesty.

"Empty nester," Nolan said. "You know what that means?"

"What's that?"

"You're free as a bird."

A low laugh rose up from Ava's chest, and she shook her head. "It doesn't feel that way."

"You could go back to school."

She shot him a look as she paused at a stop sign. His eyes met hers, so intent that it gave her pause. Then she looked away and pulled carefully out onto Highway 17.

"What for?" she asked.

"For whatever you want."

"I never wanted to go to school," Ava said in a low voice. "I wanted to travel, like you and Toni. But I wasn't brave enough. I let my mom push me into going to UCSD."

"She was set on you being the first Hoffman to go to college." Nolan's voice was just as quiet; she could barely hear him over the engine and the sound of tires on the highway.

"And I was. But Maggie was the first of us to graduate. I didn't even last three semesters."

"You took a different path."

"Sure did."

"Do you regret it?"

"I could never regret the choices that gave me my children," Ava said. "Even if their father wasn't... well, wasn't a good match for me in the long run. Maggie wasn't a mistake. She wasn't even an accident."

"You mean you... decided to have a baby?"

"At eighteen," she confirmed. "Unmarried... I hadn't even declared a college major. I thought I could just have her and go right back to class with a baby in my arms. Then I ended up a nineteen-year-old dropout, married to a military man. I was just so desperate for family that I created one. It all sounds crazy to me now. I was barely older than my son, and he's still such a baby. Though of course he thinks he's so grown up." Ava sighed.

"Hindsight," Nolan murmured. She could feel his eyes on her still, but she kept hers fixed on the highway.

"I was happy," she said quietly. "I was so young. I had so much energy. Maggie's father was gone most of the time, which suited me just fine. I had a home and food and my baby girl. She was the light of my life. Still is. So no, I can't regret any of the decisions that gave me the two most precious people in my life. Even if they were objectively crazy."

"There's nothing crazy about wanting a family. Crazy is a society that demands families scatter their teenage kids to the four winds."

"Didn't you ever want a family?" Ava asked.

"I had one."

Ava very nearly swerved into the car next to her. As far as she knew, the only family Nolan had was the closed and distant father who had moved him to Redwood Grove as a teenager and then proceeded to drink himself into an early grave. "What do you mean?"

"Toni never told you?"

She shook her head. Toni had hardly mentioned Nolan to Ava from the day he had broken her heart to the day he had moved back to Redwood Grove over twenty years later.

"It was why she took pity on me and invited me to take

over her job in Costa Rica. Okay, backing up. When I was... twenty-eight? Maybe twenty-nine? I met a woman in Bali. She was from New Zealand, and she already had two boys, twins. They were just three years old. Their father wanted nothing to do with them, but he did pay child support. It didn't stretch far in New Zealand, so she moved to Bali." He was quiet for a moment. "They called me Dad. We were together for eight years. Lived in nine different countries. I stayed with her a lot longer than I would have, honestly, if it weren't for those boys. I loved them like my own."

He was quiet for a long moment before he continued, "But they weren't mine. So when things truly went south—we wanted different things, started arguing all the time—that was it. She took the boys back to New Zealand, and there wasn't a thing that I could do to stop her. The relocation would have been one thing. We did that together plenty of times. But she completely cut me off from the boys. No visits, no phone calls... it was like I had never been in their lives at all."

"I am so sorry, Nolan. That's any parent's worst nightmare."

He nodded slowly. "Toni knew the boys. She'd met them a couple times over the years. Along with their mother, of course. She saw how lost I was after that."

"And that's how you ended up in Costa Rica."

"Costa Rica first, yeah. And then Hoffman Farm. Full circle."

"Full circle," Ava echoed as she took a looping exit off of the highway.

"I missed you," Nolan said, so quietly that Ava thought she might have imagined it.

She didn't know what to say to that.

. . .

When they walked into Gran's hospital room, Marisol was deep in conversation with one of the nurses. They were talking in Spanish, and Ava picked up just enough to understand that they were discussing what sort of care Gran would need when she was eventually discharged. They'd discussed the situation with Marisol a few days earlier, and she'd been eager to help, which was a blessing for sure. Now they just had to get Gran well enough for that to happen...

"More visitors!" Gran's face lit up at the sight of them. "Would you look at that, Tessa?" she said to the nurse. "It's a red-letter day."

Ava crossed the room and took Gran's hands between her own. "You should have told me that Marisol's a nurse."

They'd spent a few days hammering out specifics and making sure it would actually work before bringing it to Gran for approval, and she'd been thrilled. Already, the news that she'd likely be able to go home in the not-too-distant future seemed to have lifted her mood.

"I haven't exactly been in full possession of my faculties," Gran said in the same tone of mild reproach. "And I didn't want to assume that she would be willing to take care of me."

"She was happy to be asked. She loved her job back home and is looking forward to diving back in," Nolan said. "Besides, you're a national treasure. Who would say no?"

Gran reached out for him so that she was holding hands with both him and Ava at the same time. "Look at you. My babies, all grown up. And exactly the same."

"You been hitting the juice again, Gran?" Nolan made a show of peering at the IV that was hooked to her arm.

"Oh, who can keep track of what all they give me?" Gran sank back into her pillows with a restless sigh. "I've never spent so much time between four walls in my entire life. I can't wait to get out of this place. They're saying I should be ready once they get my blood pressure under control."

"Ava?" Marisol called. "I pick my daughter up from school. You stay to talk with the nurse?"

"Of course," Ava said. "Thank you so much for spending the morning with Gran. And for everything. I can't tell you how grateful I am."

Marisol responded with a modest shrug. "This is also good for me. I work with Gran instead of work the farm, and I have more time for studying. Then, when Gran is better, I have a very good reference for the kind of work that I want to do. It's what you call a win-win."

"It sure is," Ava agreed. "I still think we're getting the better side of the bargain."

"I don't know about that. I'm going to go for Lucia," Marisol said. "You talk to the nurse about what is needed."

"Of course."

Nolan chatted with Gran as Ava went through an intimidating list of things that Gran would need for in-home care. From pills to a wheelchair to a prosthetic and visits from physical therapists... without Marisol's help, it never would have been possible. Even *with* Marisol's help, paying for everything that Gran would need might be more than Ava could manage. But her savings combined with the farm earnings and hopefully the café would see Gran through after that. It was going to work out.

It had to.

"We were just talking about where to build the wheelchair ramp," Nolan said when the nurse left.

"I hate that my condition is leaving a mark on our farmhouse," Gran said with a sigh.

Ava took her hand. "Let's focus on the fact that you're coming home to that farmhouse."

"You'll need to move me into the downstairs bedroom," Gran said. "I don't want one of those ridiculous electric contraptions going up and down the stairs. The wheelchair ramp is bad enough. You and your mother can have the upstairs, and I'll take the down."

"Of course, Gran. I'll have everything set up by the time you come home."

"In the meantime," said Nolan, "what say we break you out of here for the day? Do you want to go to a restaurant?"

"Lord, no. I want to be *outside*."

"Your wish is my command," he told her. "Let me chase down someone to get you unhooked from all of this, and we'll get you some sunshine."

"That man is a treasure," Gran said as Nolan went out into the hall.

Ava held Gran's hand and watched him go. She couldn't disagree.

15

Beth

BETH HAD OFFICIALLY HIT a new low.

The shop had been empty all morning, and she had spent that time stalking her ex-boyfriend on social media. She'd wasted nearly two hours cycling between Facebook, Instagram, Snapchat, and TikTok. Not satisfied by the pictures that Josh posted himself, Beth had gone down the rabbit hole looking at photos from his new followers and people that he tagged in his stories.

While Beth sat there knitting like an old biddy, Josh was living it up all over the Bay Area. Apparently, in less than two weeks' time, he had connected with a couple old high school friends who now lived in San Francisco, and half of the photos that Beth found of him included a pretty blond girl named Jessica.

Beth's phone threw up a low battery warning in protest, and she tossed the tiny computer aside with a groan of defeat.

What was she *doing* with her life?

The bloom was off the rose, and Beth was starting to second guess every decision that she had made in the past... well, ever. The intoxicating freedom of living alone for the first time in her life had quickly faded, leaving behind a deep sense of loss. Loneliness had taken up residence in her chest, weighing her down and making each little thing that she had to do for herself feel like a Herculean task. She had yet to meet a single person her age – the demographics in Redwood Grove seemed to jump right from high schoolers to young mothers, with all of the twenty-somethings off exploring the wider world – and talking to her family all the way back in Maine only deepened her feelings of isolation.

"Building community takes time," her mom had advised her on their daily phone call. "Unless of course you wanted to come home to Cherry Blossom Point, in which case..."

So, yeah, Mom wasn't terribly helpful. Or she was, but not quite in the way that Beth needed at the moment. So she glanced around the empty shop, plugged in her phone, and went through her contacts. Maybe her Aunt Anna, photographer and world traveler extraordinaire, would have better advice.

"Hey Beth!" Anna answered on the first ring. "How's California?"

Beth smiled, instantly comforted by her aunt's cheerful voice. She put her phone on speaker and set it on the counter.

"California's beautiful," she said honestly. "I bought a state park pass, and I've been exploring in the evenings after I close up the shop." Exploring alone at the end of the day –

even though she was very careful to make it back to town before dark – was the sort of thing that might have worried her mother. But Aunt Anna had explored the whole globe alone as a nature photographer; California trails had nothing on her adventures.

"That's great, Beth!"

"How's Bluebird Bay?"

"Oh, you know. Same same. Finally starting to warm up, though I know that our slightly-above-freezing temps don't hold a candle to that California sunshine."

"The sun's powerful here for sure," Beth agreed. "I'm already working on my tan. If it's warm enough on my day off, I might try a beach day down in Santa Cruz. I went to one beach and it was still a little cool and windy, but I hear it's nicer down there."

"Sounds like you're living your best life," Anna enthused. "Exploring the West Coast, basically running a yarn store. I'm so happy for you, Beth."

"Yeah," Beth said, her voice faltering slightly. "Thanks."

There was a moment of silence, and then Anna said, "But *you* don't sound happy, kiddo. What's up?"

"Living alone is so weird, Aunt Anna," Beth admitted. "At first it was amazing and wonderful and freeing, but now it's just... it's so lonely. Is that pathetic? Shouldn't I be able to enjoy being alone?"

"Don't should yourself. You think I didn't go through some dark nights of the soul when I was alone in a shack in the rainforest or mired by the side of a muddy road? Heck, it doesn't matter where you are. Loneliness will sneak up on you. It's why I never stayed away from Bluebird Bay for long. I treated it like an obligation, but the truth is that always having a home to come back to is what let me travel all those years. And you'll always have that. Not just in Cherry Blossom Point – here too."

Beth nodded and sniffed back tears, the stress of the past month flooding to the surface. "Thank you. Maybe it would be easier if I set out to do this... but I just kind of fell into it. I don't think I would have had the courage to come out here all alone."

"Don't sell yourself short, kiddo. You're braver than you think."

"Thanks, Aunt Anna." The bell above the door clanged as a customer opened it, and Beth hurried to say, "Hey, I've gotta go. I'm at work. I'll call again soon."

"It's always good to hear from you, Beth. Take care."

"Good afternoon," said the customer with a big grin. He was close to her mom's age, not exactly their usual customer – not that Beth had really seen enough people come through here to give her a fix on their 'usual customer.' Maybe he was shopping for his wife or his mom. Maybe he just liked to knit. It was definitely a soothing hobby. She shouldn't assume.

"Welcome to Imagine Knit," Beth greeted him with a smile. "Can I help you find anything?"

The man put his elbows on the counter and leaned in. "I heard that old Yoli finally hired someone, and I didn't believe it, so I had to see it for myself." He stuck his hand out across the counter. "I'm Kevin."

She shook his hand and said, "Beth Merrill."

"I'm very pleased to meet you, Beth. What brings you to Redwood Grove? Most people your age can't wait to get out of here. They all head for San Francisco or even further afield."

"I don't love big cities," Beth said hesitantly, unsure of how to answer that question. "I wanted to explore California, and I needed a job. I saw a sign on the door here and..." She trailed off and shrugged.

"Well, we're lucky to have you. An influx of young people might just revive this place."

Beth nodded dumbly. "Were you looking for something in particular, or...?"

"Oh, just browsing." Kevin's gaze drifted down to Beth's chest. She wore a hand-knit top today, a loose blue blouse speckled with sunflowers... but she got the uncomfortable feeling that this man wasn't admiring her colorwork.

"That's a beautiful sweater," he said. "Did you make that yourself?"

Beth nodded and cleared her throat. "Yes. I put the pattern up on Ravelry."

His eyes flicked back up to meet hers with a look that was entirely too intense. "What in the world is Ravelry?"

The bell above the door chimed again, and Beth turned toward it with a jerk. She felt almost guilty. Or no, not guilty. Just kind of... gross. The guy was old enough to be her dad, and she was pretty sure he was hitting on her. So when her eyes landed on Yolanda, she felt a wash of relief.

"Hi, Miss Yolanda!" Beth greeted her with slightly overzealous enthusiasm. "I didn't know you were coming in today. It's so good to see you."

"Hey there," Yolanda greeted her. The woman's steely gaze was fixed on the man on the other side of the counter. "Kevin. What brings you in? Did your wife take up knitting?" She put the slightest emphasis on the word *wife*, and the man took a quick step back from the counter.

"No such luck," he replied, sidling toward the door. "It would make buying her gifts easier. I never know *what* to get that woman. No, my sister knits. I was thinking about sending her something for her birthday... but I still wouldn't know what to get. Your inventory is... impressive. But I think I'll come back another day."

"Or don't," Yolanda said flatly. "Either way is fine by me."

"Alrighty then, have a good one," he said, having the grace to look somewhat shamefaced as he made a hasty retreat.

Yolanda watched the door close and then shook her head. "*Maleducado,*" she muttered under her breath.

"It's good to see you," Beth said again. She hoped that Yolanda wouldn't think that she was encouraging the guy. But when the old lady turned to look at her, she seemed totally normal.

"My son and I made a trip to the grocery store. I thought I would come and check on you while he finished up. How is everything going?"

"Everything's fine," Beth said automatically. Then she bit her lip, thinking of how slow business had been since the weekend.

"Slow as usual," Yolanda stated, looking around at the well-stocked shelves. "This place was busy once. People don't like to make things anymore. It doesn't help that this is the slowest time of year. The sun is finally out, and people are in no need of wool. I should maybe think of cutting back to weekend hours in the summertime."

Beth bit her lip. She couldn't make a living on weekend hours. Though she supposed that if Yolanda were still willing to give her free rent in exchange for working weekends, she could pick up a second job easily enough. But she didn't *want* a second job. She wanted to work in a happy, bustling yarn shop in this lovely little town.

"I've been thinking about teaching a class," Beth volunteered. Yolanda turned to look at her, her face impassive. "Just a beginner's class, to start. As a way of pulling in new customers. And if that goes well, I could teach more advanced classes too."

"There may not be much interest," Yolanda said. "People don't want to pay to learn to knit."

"I could teach for free," Beth volunteered. "During store hours. All they'd have to do is buy their first needles and a skein of yarn here as the cost of entry."

"You want to teach for *free?*" Yolanda asked quietly, as if she wasn't sure she'd heard her right.

"I want to earn my keep," Beth said. "I'm just sitting here all day."

"Yes, I know the feeling." Was that a trace of a smile? "It does get tedious after a while."

"I could teach a few classes at once, each based around a different project. That way, people could come to one or to all of them, whatever they like. At least one of the projects – probably a couple – will be easy enough for beginning knitters, and then I can also offer to teach colorwork and cables and such. We'll see if we can pull in anyone who used to knit but hasn't picked up their needles in a while."

"It's a good idea, Beth."

"I can make a sign and post it across the street at the grocery store." There was a colorful community bulletin board that would do nicely. "And I can post online as well, local Facebook groups and stuff. Maybe I'll even post in Half

Moon Bay and Santa Cruz, see if we can pull some more people in on the weekends."

"How'd I get so lucky to have a girl like you walk in off the street?" Yolanda asked. "You know I was thinking of selling this place?"

"I like this job, Miss Yolanda," Beth said. "I'd like to keep it."

Yolanda nodded. "You put out those signs. I'll put out word to *mis viejitas*. And print out an extra sign for me to take to the senior center."

"I will. And I was thinking about reaching out to the school, too. See if we might get in some middle schoolers or something. I know a teenager who might like to help with the class, and anything that an older girl does always seems cool to kids."

"Get them while they're young!" Yolanda chuckled. "I like it."

A man waved at her through the window, and Yolanda waved him off.

"*Ya, ya, ahorita vengo*," she called. With a wink to Beth she said, "We'll save this place yet."

"Yes!" Beth agreed. Well, she'd certainly try.

"And Beth?" Yolanda said with one hand on the door.

"Yes?"

"The next time a man comes in ogling you, just throw him right out. Take a lunch break and lock up if you'd like. Or just call me. I want you to feel safe here. You are more important than the yarn we sell, understood?"

Beth blinked back tears, startled once again by the woman's kindness. "Thank you."

Yolanda waved away her thanks. "*De nada.* Now get those posters made."

"Right away, boss," she agreed cheerfully, already feeling a renewed sense of hope.

If she could make this work, she could stay here in this town, surrounded by yarn and nature and all the things she loved. It was already starting to feel like home, and she wasn't ready to let that go.

Not without a fight.

16

Ava

IT WAS early evening by the time they tucked Gran back into her hospital bed, and she was out like a light. Gran had enjoyed every moment of her reprieve from her room at the hospital, especially when Nolan had lifted her in his arms and set her down on the grass. Gran had leaned against a broad tree trunk and stared blissfully up at the spring-green leaves that danced with sunbeams in the breeze. And when the day had started to cool and they had bundled her back into Ava's car, she was too tired and content to protest.

"I'm not eager to fight rush hour traffic on our way out of San Jose," Ava murmured as they took the elevator down to the ground floor of the hospital. She looked up at Nolan. "Do you have time to grab some food before we go?"

"I have all the time in the world," he said.

"Any suggestions on where to go? I don't know San Jose at all."

"There's a good Thai place..." Nolan pulled out his phone and typed in a name. "Yeah, it's less than a mile from here. We don't even have to get in the car. This time of day it'll be quicker to walk."

"Sounds perfect," Ava said.

The walk and their meal were filled with comfortable conversation, getting to know each other again after so many years apart. Nolan told story after story about his years abroad and the piece of his heart that was still missing, the two boys he had helped to raise.

"They're seventeen now." Nolan shook his head slowly, as if he couldn't quite believe it.

"Wow," Ava murmured. "The same age as my son. That's such a trip, Nolan. I can't believe I never knew about them."

One of his eyebrows quirked up a bit. "I did try to friend you on Facebook a time or two."

Ava looked away, hoping that the blush that rose to her cheeks wasn't too obvious.

"One of the boys actually found me there just a couple of days ago."

"Really?" Ava said, looking back at Nolan. "How are they?"

"They seem to be doing well. I guess they settled into a more conventional life when their mom moved them back to New Zealand. They've been going to school, living with a stepdad and two little sisters."

"Oh wow," Ava murmured. "Was that hard to hear?"

"I don't mind that she's moved on, if that's what you mean. I hope she's happy. But it still stings that I couldn't be there for those boys through their teen years, after all the time we spent together. They like their stepdad fine, he's not a bad guy or anything, but they aren't close. Bodhi just didn't have much to say about him."

"And you're only in contact with one of the boys?"

Nolan was quiet for a moment, picking listlessly at his curry. "I think Zen still resents me for not being there for them. For not... I don't know. Following them back. Fighting harder, somehow. Or maybe I'm just projecting. Maybe he just doesn't care about his mom's old boyfriend that he hasn't seen since he was eleven."

"Three to eleven is a long time."

"Yeah," Nolan sighed. "And we spent more time together than most families. They went to school a few times, but there were long stretches – whole countries, you know? – that they weren't in school at all. We were just together all the time."

"I'm so sorry that you were separated from your kids, Nolan."

"They were never mine," he said shortly.

"I know, but–"

"Traffic's probably cleared now." Nolan looked up at her with a smile. "Should we head out?"

Ava blinked at him for a moment, shaken by the swift change of topic, but then she nodded. "Sure."

It was clearly a sore spot, and she wasn't about to push it.

They talked about lighter things on the walk back to the car and the long drive back to the farm. When they were nearly home, a sudden flash of gold in the darkness made Ava wonder if she was seeing things.

"Was that...?"

"Phoenix!" Nolan exclaimed. "What in the... we must be nearly two miles from the farm! I know I shut the gate."

"Let me find a safe place to pull over and we'll get him."

"There's a spot just up the road."

"Yeah, I see it." Ava parked in a small bit of dirt between the road and the cliffside, just big enough for her car.

"I'll get him," Nolan said. He climbed out and circled around, looking up and down the road for oncoming traffic. Then he called, "Phoenix! Here, boy!"

Phoenix just barked at him and bounced from side to side like he wanted Nolan to chase him down the road.

Nolan crouched down and called, "Phoenix! Come!"

Phoenix barked again, looking very happy with himself. Nolan tried to grab him, but Phoenix danced away.

"Of all the..." Nolan muttered, looking up and down the road again. Like most stretches of this road, they were between two blind turns. He walked to the car and opened one of the back doors. "Phoenix, car ride! Come here, boy!"

The golden retriever perked up at that, and finally he trotted toward the car.

Just then, a car came tearing around the curve, going a good twenty miles per hour above the road's speed limit. Nolan tried to call the dog, tried to wave at the car to get their attention, but it was too little too late. The car headlights shone bright on his face, and for a horrified moment Ava thought that the car might hit *him*.

Phoenix startled and tried to jump out of the way, but the corner of the car caught him right in his side. He flew through the air as tires screeched on the mountain road.

Nolan rushed to the dog and knelt in the road, looking down at him. Ava jumped out of her car and ran to them.

"What the hell?" shouted the driver who had hit Phoenix. "What the hell was that dog doing in the middle of the road?"

Ava turned her back on the stranger and crouched down by Phoenix, who looked her straight in the eye with a fear and pleading that broke her heart. Nolan tried to lift him, and Phoenix yelped in pain. Nolan cursed under his breath.

"Let's try together," Ava said. "Just a sec."

She ran to her car and opened the hatchback, then went back to slide her hands beneath the dog. Another car came around the bend, but the man who had hit Phoenix stepped out in front of it, blocking traffic. Together, Ava and Nolan formed a sort of stretcher with their arms and carried Phoenix to her car, where they eased him onto the back of Ava's CRV.

"The vet in Redwood Grove is closest," Nolan said.

"It's nearly seven," Ava protested even as she turned the car around and went back the way they had just come. "They won't be open."

"They'll be open for us," Nolan said, bringing his phone up to his ear. "Hello? Yeah. Phoenix was just hit by a car. Yeah, ten minutes or so. Okay, thanks."

"They're there?"

"They will be. The vet lives in town, not far from the clinic."

"Good," Ava said, too panicked and focused on driving to think of anything else to say.

Nolan turned in his seat to look at Phoenix. "Hang in there, buddy."

. . .

They sat in the empty waiting room at the vet's office for an hour. Ava's hand was clasped tightly in Nolan's as they waited silently for news. Even in the middle of the chaos and worry, Ava couldn't help but marvel at how *right* that felt. Simply sitting there, side by side. Hand in hand.

"Phoenix is going to be okay," the vet told them before the door had even swung shut behind her.

"Does he need surgery?" Nolan asked. Even as they stood, he held Ava's hand fast in his.

"Probably not. He has several fractured ribs, but none of them are fully broken. As long as you can keep him calm and inactive, they should heal fine on their own. Too much exercise too soon and you risk one of those ribs cracking, even injuring his lungs. But we'll send you home with sedatives and pain meds, and he should be okay."

"How long will it take for him to heal?"

"It could be a month or two. The first couple weeks are the most critical. Just keep him warm and make sure he doesn't get dehydrated. Wet food is good, or even broth. I'll show you which ribs are fractured and help you get him to the car."

"Thank you," Nolan said.

"What do we owe you?" asked Ava.

"Oh, nothing," the vet said, waving her question away. "How's your grandmother?"

"Much improved, thank you. She'll be coming home soon."

"I'm glad to hear it. Come on through."

. . .

Ava drove at half speed on the way home to the farmhouse, taking the turns of the windy mountain road extra slowly and going five miles an hour over the bumps of the dirt road. Nolan let out a low growl when he saw that the back gate to the farm was still open, but he got out and closed it behind them without saying a word.

He did a quick headcount after Ava parked and they got out of the car.

"The rest of the dogs are still here." He opened the back of the car and stroked Phoenix's head.

"That's good," Ava murmured, running up the porch steps to open the door and then hurrying back down to help carry Phoenix up to the house. But Nolan had already eased the big dog into his arms with a minimum of whimpers and whines, so Ava stepped aside and let him carry the golden retriever up the stairs on his own.

Inside, Nolan set Phoenix down gently on a big dog bed near Gran's old cast-iron stove. He glanced at his watch and said, "He's still an hour out from his next dose of meds."

"I've got them in my purse," Ava said, "and I already set an alarm on my phone to give him more in the middle of the night so that he doesn't wake up in pain."

"I hadn't even thought about that," Nolan said. "You shouldn't be waking up in the middle of the night. He's not even your dog. I can take him to my place if you want."

"No," Ava said immediately. "Let's not move the poor guy again. Not yet. I don't mind getting up. I rarely sleep all the way through the night anyway. I'll probably be awake. I just set the alarm to make sure."

"If you say so..." Nolan went back to the dog and patted him gently, keeping his hand far away from Phoenix's injured ribs. "They gave him IV fluids at the clinic. But we should see if he'll at least take some water in the morning."

"I have a bunch of bones in the freezer," Ava told him. "I'll make some broth overnight. Just for him, with no onions or garlic. And I have turkey lunch meat in the fridge."

Nolan looked up at her with a soft smile. "You're amazing."

His eyes held hers long enough for the air between them to start to feel charged, and then he cleared his throat and looked away.

"It's supposed to get cold tonight. Okay by you if I start a fire in the wood stove?"

"That would be great," Ava said. "Thank you."

"No problem," Nolan said. "Wood's a bit low. I'll bring some in from outside in case you want to add more in the wee hours. You remember how? This side door, here?"

"I remember," she said softly.

He met her eyes and looked away quickly, nodding. "I don't imagine there are wood stoves in San Diego."

"Not that I've seen." Ava was quiet for a moment, watching him start the fire. "It never felt quite like a proper home without one. A house, sure. But nothing like this farmhouse." She sighed and looked around at the familiar boards of her childhood home. "This place groans when the wind picks up, and the floorboards creek underfoot, but somehow, it feels so much more solid than any of the houses I've lived in down in SoCal. Those new builds have no soul."

When she looked back at Nolan, he was staring at her with a look she couldn't fathom. His face seemed to change in the flickering light of the growing fire. One second he looked sixty, and the next moment she caught a glimpse of him at sixteen. Then he closed the glass door, and his face settled back into itself. Forty-three. Too young for her. Too old for games.

The gulf between men and women in their forties was so unfair, thought Ava as he stepped outside for more firewood. As teenagers, they had been a perfect match. Or at least she had thought so. But at forty-three? Ava was already an empty-nester. At any moment, she could become a grandmother. Nolan was the exact same age, but he was a man. Still young enough to start a family, if that's what he wanted. And didn't he deserve that? The chance to have children of his own?

But God, the way he looked at her sometimes... She wasn't imagining that, was she? The look in his eyes, the electricity between them....

This is what had kept her away for so long. The fear of that chemistry. That it would still be there, or that it wouldn't. Ava wasn't sure which possibility was more terrifying.

"This should be more than enough for tonight and tomorrow," Nolan said as he came in with an armful of wood and dropped it in its place beside the stove. "I'll bring more in when you run low."

"Thank you." Ava sat beside Phoenix, letting the stove warm her. The dog put his muzzle on her leg and settled into a fitful sleep.

Nolan hovered by the door as if uncertain of whether he should stay or go. Ava looked up at him.

"Sit with us for a while?" she said.

"Gladly." He settled down next to her, looking into the fire. Ava studied his face, noting the things that had changed.

The scruff along his jaw that came in so much thicker than it had when they were kids. A long, thin scar at his temple that cut into his hairline. Such small things. The truth was, he was still so much the same. His smile, his heart, the curve of his jaw. Each one just as she'd remembered them.

"Can I ask you something?" Ava murmured.

Nolan looked at her and nodded, his face serious in the firelight.

"Why did you break up with me?" The moment that she uttered the question, Ava felt such a flood of vulnerability and regret that she pressed her eyes shut. "I'm sorry. I know it's ancient history. It was a lifetime ago. I just..." She opened her eyes and took a breath. She couldn't bring herself to look him in the face, so she stared through the glass window at the small fire that flared in the stove. "I'll be honest, Nolan. It's always haunted me. The great unanswered question of my life. One moment we were so in love... or, well, I was. And we were talking about the future, about taking that truck of yours cross country and working on farms and seeing the world. And then..." She trailed off and swallowed.

Then the beautiful boy she'd loved with her whole young heart and soul had pulled her aside on their last day of high school to tell her that he was leaving town. Alone. No explanation. Just a world of pain and regret in his eyes that belied his words: "It's better this way."

"It's not," Ava had said. She had been so shocked, so heartbroken that those two small words were the only argument she had been able to utter. "It's not."

"We'll still be friends, won't we?" he had asked, his voice on the verge of breaking.

She had just shaken her head, mute. Nolan had walked

away and left town without even walking in their graduation ceremony. And Ava hadn't seen him for twenty-six years.

Nolan was quiet for so long that Ava thought he might not answer. But at long last he said, "You had a scholarship."

She turned to look at him, bewildered. "What?"

"You had a full ride to UC San Diego." His face was so close to hers, the look in his eyes a strange blend of affection and frustration. "And when I didn't get in, you were going to give it up to drive across the country with me in that thirty-year-old truck... you know I didn't even make it out of California before the thing broke down?"

Ava shook her head slowly, holding his eyes with hers. They looked dark green in the firelight, more forest than water. He looked away and let out a breath of air that was almost a laugh.

"My dad told me that if I really loved you, I would let you go."

"I didn't care about college," she murmured. "I wanted to go with you."

"It felt wrong to let you abandon your scholarship like that."

"You could have come with me."

Nolan looked at her again, his gaze intense. "I should have."

And then he kissed her.

His hand, broad and strong from the daily work of running the farm, gently cradled the side of her jaw. Ava didn't know how long they sat like that, lost in each other, but they jumped away like guilty teenagers when the kitchen door swung open.

"Oh!" Lyra exclaimed. "You scared me! What are you doing on the kitchen floor?"

"Phoenix was hit by a car," Ava said as they rose to their feet.

"The dog?" Lyra asked blankly.

"Yes, the dog. Did you close the gate when you came in?"

"Of course I closed the gate."

"I should go," Nolan said. "I'll be back in the morning to check on Phoenix."

"I'll walk you out," Ava told him. She followed him out onto the back porch and closed the door firmly behind them. He turned and looked at her for a long moment. Then he chuckled, a low sound deep in his chest, and she watched the tension release from his shoulders. He leaned down and planted a solid kiss on her lips, one hand on the back of her head... and then he stepped away.

"Good night, Ava."

She realized that she was holding her fingertips to her lips. She let her hand drop and gave him a bashful smile, feeling like a kid again. He was already gone when she finally managed to whisper her reply.

"Good night, Nolan."

17

Toni

TONI SHIVERED as she hurried through the hospital. The labyrinth of identical hallways felt like something out of a horror movie... albeit a brightly lit horror movie. The place tried to make up for the lack of windows with glaring fluorescent lights that gave Toni an instant headache.

She hated everything about this place. She hated fighting through traffic to get here. She hated the smell of antiseptic and the droning buzz and beeps of various machines.

Only her love for Gran kept her coming back time and again, armed with a fresh bouquet of flowers and a thermos of tea. Today, the bouquet and the tea were made with the same mix of plants. Each one was mostly calendula with a smattering of fennel, lemon balm, and echinacea. The purple coneflowers of the echinacea were a gorgeous contrast with the bright orange calendula. The tea was sweet and mellow but fortifying.

Finally, after a number of wrong turns and a useless lap around the wrong side of the building, Toni found the right room. Gran was dozing, half reclined in her hospital bed, so Toni quietly set about replacing a wilting group of daffodils with her fresh bouquet.

"Toni," Gran greeted her with a smile, still half awake. "Aren't you a sweetheart. Look at those."

"When we can't bring Gran to the garden, we bring the garden to Gran." Toni kissed her on the forehead and poured her a cup of tea.

"No Juniper today?" Gran pushed a button that brought the back of her bed up a bit more. She accepted the tea and breathed in the fragrant steam.

"She wanted to come, but she's busy watching her little cousins." Babysitting Lizzie's girls was one act of many that made Toni wish that Juniper could stay forever. Toni loved her little nieces, but there were times that helping Lizzie out felt like a full-time job. Toni wanted to help her little sister, she did. Being a single mom was brutally hard... but that's why Toni had been so careful to avoid that fate, so careful to build a life for herself that was entirely hers. She was happy to help with the girls here and there, but she couldn't be a second mother to them at the expense of her business.

Juniper was something else entirely, basically an adult. She pulled her own weight and then some. The time that Toni spent teaching Juniper the ins and outs of her small business was repaid in full by the hours that Juniper put in. Toni would be happy to keep her oldest niece around forever – not that Ethan would let her.

"How *is* Juniper? Has she been to see her mother?"

Toni shook her head. "She hasn't even mentioned her."

"Well, I can hardly blame her." Gran sighed and took a sip of tea. "This is delicious, Toni. Thank you."

"I'm worried about Jun," Toni admitted. "She wants to skip out on the rest of the school year, but her dad already let her stay way longer than he'd wanted. My gut says she should be here with me right now, but maybe that's just me being selfish. I love having her around. But I'm worried that I'm not doing her any favors, letting her hide from her problems. I wonder if I should just bite the bullet, side with her dad, and tell her to go and finish out the school year."

"And how does Juniper feel about all that?"

"She's adamant that she's not going back. I'm half afraid that she'd hitchhike right out of Santa Cruz again."

"So why push?" Gran asked.

"She's a minor. Am I not supposed to push her to do the right thing?"

"Is going back to Santa Cruz High the right thing for *her*?"

Toni suddenly pictured Juniper at an under-sized desk in a concrete block, listlessly sketching weeds under fluorescent lights as a teacher droned on Charlie Brown style: *wahwahwahwahwah.* Then she pictured Juniper in the garden, at the farmers market, running down the beach with her little cousins – all lit up.

"Ethan thinks so," she said weakly. "He thinks she should at least finish out the year."

Gran gave her a long look over her mug of herbal tea. "If Juniper were thirty and in a bad marriage or a job that she hated, would you tell her to stay? How long? Till her next promotion? Anniversary? Death do them part?"

Toni shook her head. "Of course not."

"And yet that's what kids are supposed to do. Suck it up, even when they're miserable, because that's the way we've always done it. It was hard enough for me, being stuck under a roof all day when I just wanted to be home on the farm running through the fields or climbing trees in our orchard... and our little old Redwood Grove schoolhouse was idyllic compared to some. Not everyone is cut out to be in a classroom all day. The headlines talk about mental health crises in youth as if the cause were some great mystery. Not everyone learns the same way. Not everyone thrives the same way..."

"I hated the classroom," she acknowledged. "I felt like a wild thing in a cage. Ava helped keep me sane, and school in Redwood Grove wasn't too bad. We were able to eat lunch outside, at least. I have friends on the East Coast who tell me their kids eat in a lunchroom in the basement every day, even when it's sunny and warm. That's mind-boggling to me."

Gran took a deep breath, looking out the hospital window at the gray parking lot beyond. "Sixteen-year-olds used to dig into their home soil and grow crops. They had the option to learn a useful trade or climb ship rigging and see distant shores. Now they're just supposed to memorize brick after brick of information that half of them forget over summer. And the people in charge pretend that at the end of it all, they've built something worthwhile. When really, all some kids are left with is a pile of broken bricks. I've seen Juniper in the garden. She's radiant."

"She is," Toni acknowledged.

"Don't take that away from her. She belongs out there in the sunlight."

"Gran, you're preaching to the choir. But she's not my daughter."

"No, she's her own person. With a right to her own decisions."

"Morally, yes. I'm with you. But legally..." Toni shrugged. "She's still sixteen. She's barely sixteen. Her dad has to agree."

"So get him to agree," Gran said. "You have more pull with the Flores clan than you think. You're their matriarch, like it or not."

"Isn't Patricia the matriarch?" Toni asked.

Gran snorted. "Your stepmother is a good woman, in her own way. But no. Your siblings look up to you, Toni. All of them. Their kids adore you. And Juniper in particular thinks you hung the moon."

"No pressure."

"Oh, it's plenty of pressure. But family is worth it."

She blew out a noisy breath and stood to pour Gran another cup of tea. "Life was simpler when I lived three thousand miles away from all of them."

Gran gave her a knowing smile. "Was it?"

She thought back to the farm in Costa Rica, her string of new-age boyfriends, and a revolving door of mostly useless volunteers. Then she met Gran's eyes and smiled. "Not really."

Her phone buzzed. She pulled it from her pocket and saw Ethan's name, then turned the screen to show Gran. "Speak of the devil."

"Your little brother isn't the devil."

"It's a figure of speech, Gran."

She continued like she hadn't heard her. "He's lost and in need of guidance. He wants to do right by his daughter. He just doesn't know what that looks like."

"Who am I to tell him how to parent?"

"Not you. Juniper. She knows what she needs. Help him listen to her."

"I'll try." She pocketed her phone without answering, done with this conversation for now. "How's your blood pressure?"

"Getting better every day."

"Have you eaten yet?"

Gran pressed her lips together in a flat frown. "They brought by something that they claimed were eggs but most definitely came out of a box. Along with a bagel that resembled a rock."

"That's grim."

"I ate a bit of lime Jell-O."

"That's something." Toni pulled her phone back out, swiping past the missed call to look at delivery options. "Breakfast is a bit sparse, but there's a grocery store just down the road. I bet they have a hot bar full of breakfast stuff."

"I'd kill for some potato salad."

Toni put her phone down and smiled at Gran. "A hot breakfast and a tub of potato salad for lunch, coming right up."

"And then you'll call your brother back," she said, a statement of fact.

She sighed and wrinkled her nose. Gran made it sound so simple, but the reality was that she and Juniper had used up the last of Ethan's patience. He was going to drag Juni back to Santa Cruz, and there wasn't a thing that Toni could do about it. But still, she had to try.

"Yeah. And then I'll call Ethan."

God help her.

18

Ava

THERE WAS a light rap on the kitchen door at dawn, just after Ava gave Phoenix a dose of meds wrapped in sliced turkey. She went to open it, and a jolt went through her at the sight of Nolan, who was wearing a faded plaid shirt and a shy smile.

"Good morning," Ava said, frozen in the doorway.

"You're up," he said with some relief.

"I am. And Phoenix is doing as well as can be. I just gave him his pills."

"Good. That's good." Nolan cleared his throat and gestured to a table saw he had set up near the house. "If you don't mind some noise, I'd like to start work on a ramp."

"A ramp," Ava repeated blankly.

"Gran will need one when she gets home," he explained, and a rush of something dangerously close to love washed over her. She wasn't ready to fall for Nolan Pasternak again, not when they still lived so far apart. But she had nearly forgotten what it felt like to have someone looking out for her and her family, standing beside her and helping her to shoulder the work of the day.

"I already have all the materials," he continued. "But I figured that if I build it now, Phoenix can get in and out of the house when he needs to pee. The vet said no jumping, and the porch steps seem like they'd be a bit beyond him right now. I can carry him down and up again and then start work on the ramp."

"Okay." Ava backed out of his way. "Sure. Thank you."

"Of course." Nolan walked into the kitchen, and Phoenix's golden tail beat excitedly against the tile floor. He started to get up and then slumped back to the floor in pain, but his tail never stopped.

"Maybe give him some time for the pain meds to kick in?" Ava suggested as Nolan scratched Phoenix's head. "I just gave them to him, so he might be hurting right now."

"Good call," Nolan said. "I'll see if I can set up a temporary ramp for him in the meantime."

"Are you hungry?" Ava asked.

Nolan paused with one hand on the kitchen door and turned to her with a faint smile. "I had a piece of toast with my coffee, but I wouldn't turn down a second breakfast."

"I'll see what I can scrounge up."

"Thank you."

When Ava went outside with a cup of chai and an egg sandwich, Nolan was finishing up his impromptu ramp.

"Very impressive," she said, holding out her breakfast offering.

"It won't do for Gran, but it will get Phoenix out before he pees on the floor." Nolan whistled. "Here, boy!"

Phoenix came through the door at a pace between a walk and a run. His movements were stiff and painful, but his tail moved as happily as ever as he made his way down the ramp and out into the weedy yard. Nolan sat in one of the porch chairs, and Ava joined him with her own breakfast. As they sat there, eating quietly, Phoenix hobbled up the ramp and flumped back down in the kitchen.

"That ramp is a lifesaver," Ava said.

"It's just a placeholder. It shouldn't take long to build a sturdy one for Gran."

"Thank you for that."

"It's my pleasure." Nolan paused, looking like he wanted to say something more, but then he just smiled and set down his empty plate. "Thanks for the sandwich."

Ava nodded, watching as he went down to the yard and started measuring and marking the lumber he'd brought. Then she shook herself out of it and went inside, back to her own work.

Not long after the saw started up, Lyra came into the kitchen with a dramatic groan. "*What* is that racket?"

"Nolan's building a ramp for Gran," Ava told her.

Lyra grunted in acknowledgement, still looking aggrieved. "Is there coffee?"

"Yeah." Ava poured her a cup and handed it over. Lyra drank it black, and then set it down still half full.

"I can't even hear myself think. I'm going to the Redwood House for breakfast, and then I'm going to visit your grandmother. Do you want to come?"

"Thanks, but I already ate. I'm going to stay here and finish putting in orders for the café."

Lyra sighed, giving Ava a long look. When she did that, Ava always felt uncomfortably aware of how Lyra's bright blue eyes were nearly identical to her own. Sometimes meeting her mother's eyes felt like looking into a funhouse mirror.

"Don't go investing everything you have into that old café," Lyra said at last. "The place closed for a reason."

Ava turned away to pour herself a second cup of coffee. "Tell Gran I'll be there tomorrow morning."

"Okay." Lyra sounded sad, and it was a long time before she turned to go. But whatever was on her mother's mind, Ava just didn't have the time or the energy for it right now. She didn't even have the mental space to wonder about last night's kiss with Nolan and what it meant.

She was going to finish the orders for the Hoffman Café. And that place *was* going to bring in enough money to pay for Gran's care. It had to.

Late afternoon sun slanted through the kitchen windows by the time that a knock on the door distracted Ava from the numbers in front of her. She had spent most of the day on the phone with local vendors before switching over to the pile of notes and figures that comprised her somewhat messy business plan. Ava thumped Gran's jasper paperweight down on top of the pile and rose with a sigh. Under better circumstances, she would probably enjoy reviving the old café. But now, with this ridiculous timeline and Gran's livelihood on the line... it felt a lot like bailing water out of a sinking ship.

"How's our patient?" Nolan asked when Ava opened the kitchen door.

"Overdue for a pee break, probably." Ava felt a twinge of guilt as she watched Phoenix struggle to his feet and limp toward the door, tail wagging despite his broken ribs. He had been so quiet all day that she had nearly forgotten he was there. Only the alarms she'd set on her phone ensured that he got his pills and sliced turkey at regular intervals. Ava herself hadn't eaten a thing since breakfast.

"I'm just in time, then." Nolan stepped aside and let Phoenix walk down the newly constructed wheelchair ramp. "I'll add a railing before Gran comes home, but the ramp is sound."

"It looks fantastic, Nolan. Thank you."

"It's nothing." He ran a hand through his auburn hair and gave Ava a crooked smile. "Have you eaten? I thought we might drive over to that new restaurant in Davenport."

"I'd like that," Ava said, not giving herself a chance to overthink the invitation. "I'll just get Phoenix settled, and we can go."

Ava climbed into Nolan's truck, and they drove down the One. Nolan didn't tell her where they were going, and Ava didn't ask. She was content to sit and listen to the obscure rock bands that Nolan favored, watching the California coast flit by out her window.

When they reached Davenport, he parked in front of a restaurant she had never seen before. *La Toscana* was housed in a two-story building, and the staff greeted Nolan by name as he led her through the restaurant and up the stairs.

"Come here a lot?" Ava asked as she followed him to the second floor.

"Every week." Nolan shot her a grin over his shoulder. "We grow parsley for them and some other things depending on the season."

They had only just sat down at an ocean-view table when a waitress appeared with a bottle of wine and two glasses. As she opened the bottle, she said, "Your food will be ready any minute."

Ava gave Nolan a questioning look, and he winked at her.

"I texted the chef in advance," he said.

"Oh." Ava wasn't sure how she felt about him ordering for her, but she could roll with it. Maybe the chef was making them something special. The way that Nolan was looking at her was almost too much, new and familiar at the same time, and she looked out over the water as she sipped her (admittedly delicious) wine.

The waitress was back a moment later, carrying two identical bowls. Bits of toasted bread mingled with cut vegetables, and the tangy dressing hit Ava's nose as their server set the bowls on the table. Her eyes went wide, and she looked at Nolan, who was watching her with an expectant grin.

"No way," Ava breathed.

"Yes way."

"Panzanella."

"Panzanella," Nolan confirmed.

She carefully put together a bite of toasted bread, cucumber, and heirloom tomato. Nolan watched as she put it in her mouth and chewed. Instantly, the tang of onion and basil transported her back to those carefree summer days when she and Nolan were joined at the hip.

"It tastes just like I remember," she told him.

"It's the same chef. He tried to retire when he closed the place in Redwood Grove, but he got bored. So when a friend opened this place and asked him to run the kitchen, he accepted."

Ava shook her head in wonder and took another bite. When she and Nolan were young and in love, the only thing that they could afford on most of their dates to the local Italian restaurant was a shared bowl of panzanella. It became their summer staple, fresh and filling.

She felt Nolan's eyes on her and looked up from her food. Ava watched him watching her, and his cheeks colored slightly. He looked down and picked up his own fork.

"This is perfect," she told him.

"This is only the start of the evening." He met her eyes again, looking as sweet and shy as he had as a kid. "If you're free?"

Ava smiled at him. "What did you have in mind?"

He shook his head and gave her a cheeky grin. "It's a surprise."

The rest of the meal passed with easy conversation, two friends catching up after years apart. No longer being strapped teenagers, they followed the small bowls of panzanella with mushroom soup and braised lamb. The check, quickly snatched up by Nolan, was accompanied by two perfect ricciarelli biscuits. Powdered sugar melted on Ava's tongue as she bit into the soft almond cookie. Nolan watched her with a gratified expression and pushed the second cookie in her direction.

"So?" she asked, licking the last of the powdered sugar from her fingertips. "What's next?"

"It's a surprise," Nolan said again.

Ava scrunched up her nose at him, but he just beamed at her and started for the stairs. The sun approached the horizon as they drove back up the One, and Nolan pulled off to the side of the road.

"Is this the surprise?" she asked as the blue sky gave way to pink and gold.

Nolan shook his head. "Just a detour."

They were quiet as they watched the colors in the clouds intensify. Nolan took Ava's hand, and she let him. She didn't know what she was doing, or where this was going, or how long she could stay... but God, it felt good to have her hand in his again.

His fingers had been just as long as this when he was a lanky teenager, his hand engulfing hers. But his hands were more muscular now, the skin pleasantly rough from his work in the fields. Ava's mind wandered to how those hands might feel elsewhere, and she quickly forced those thoughts to retreat. Not that she was opposed to the idea, exactly... but she had enough to worry about right now without letting things move so far so fast.

In that moment, just being there next to him was enough.

She had dreamed of moments like this. Quite literally dreamed of them. Ava would be going through the motions of her life as a wife and mother, would successfully go for weeks or even months without thinking about her first love... and then *boom,* out of nowhere, he would appear in her dreams. And more often than not, the dreams were so *simple.* Just sitting together like this. And yet they had haunted her, because in those dreams, she tasted a contentment so complete and perfect that it left her real life feeling hollow. She had never felt that way with her husband. Not once.

When the last colors of the sunset drained away, Nolan gently pulled his hand from hers and started the truck. He drove through the automatic front gate of Hoffman Farm and parked behind one of the whitewashed farm cottages... his house. Nerves fluttered in Ava's chest as she began to wonder just what sort of surprise Nolan had in mind.

"Stay there," he told her, his voice warm with anticipation.

"Okay," she said uncertainly. Nolan hopped down from the cab and ran into his house, then emerged a minute later carrying a smallish black box. He crouched in front of his truck and fiddled for a moment, and then bright colors exploded on the back wall of the whitewashed cabin.

He had created their own personal drive-in.

How many nights had they spent at the local drive-in as teenagers? Sometimes they had gone in a big group or doubled with Toni and whomever she was dating at the time. And some nights it had been just the two of them in the back of his dad's old truck.

When the drive-in finally went out of business, even though Ava no longer lived in town and Nolan was long gone, it had felt like the death of a friend.

Nolan climbed back into the truck and gave her a boyish grin before settling in next to her. Ava looked back at the screen and laughed in surprise as *The Music Man* started up on the projector. Nolan clicked on a tiny portable speaker and set it on the dashboard as the train conductor onscreen called, "All aboard!"

"You remembered my favorite movie," Ava said breathlessly. Nolan gave her a long look, his expression unreadable in the faint light that flickered through the windshield.

"I remember everything," he said at last, his voice serious.

Ava leaned in and kissed him, resting one hand on his jaw as she pulled him closer to her. Then she nestled into him and turned back to the movie, watching with childlike delight as Robert Preston appeared onscreen. Nolan settled one arm around her, and for the second time that day, Ava felt perfectly and completely content.

If only for a moment.

19

Toni

"Careful!" Juniper scooped her littlest cousin up just before she collided with a huge, prickly plant. "That one will stick you!"

Kylie laughed, legs still trying to run several inches above the ground. Her big sister, Harper, sidled up to Juniper and narrowed her eyes at the towering borage.

"Why does Auntie Toni grow sharp plants?"

"It's good for the bees. Look at all those beautiful flowers."

"Purple stars!" Kylie reached out to touch them, and Juniper took another step back before setting her down.

"Exactly. That's why it's also known as the starflower."

"Lots of plants are good for bees." Harper crossed her arms over her chest and looked at the rough, weedy-looking plant with distaste. "And they're prettier. And they don't prickle."

"You're a bit prickly yourself today," Juniper teased. "Borage is good for the soil, and it helps protect the other plants from bugs that want to eat them. Plus, you can eat it. Look, you can pick the flowers without getting pricked if you're careful."

"I want a flower!" Kylie said.

"The stems and leaves are where you have to be cautious. But if you hold the flower in the middle, like this, you can pick them without getting pricked." Juniper plucked two flowers and gave one to each girl.

"It tastes like cucumber!"

Harper nibbled a microscopic bit of petal and wrinkled her nose. "I don't like it."

"Fair enough. At least you gave it a shot."

Toni smiled over her patch of lemon balm, a green carpet in the middle of the garden. Juniper had been reading some of Toni's books, and she was thrilled at all her niece had been retaining. She was thriving here, and there were whole days that the shadows in her eyes seemed to have disappeared. Of course, they still came back at moments, but definitely fewer and farther between.

They were making progress.

Toni watched as little Harper maintained her too-cool-for-borage stance of crossed arms, narrowed eyes, and a scrunched-up nose, but a smile tugged at the edge of her mouth as Juniper sank to one knee and presented her with a handful of the blue-violet flowers. Toni ducked her head, letting her sunhat hide her grin, and kept gathering lemon balm.

A car came crunching up the drive a minute later, and the two blondies ran off down the garden path with Juniper just behind them. Toni hooked her basket full of lemon balm over one arm and stood to follow, but she was distracted on her way out by a patch of weeds that were threatening to overwhelm her dill.

"My babies!" Lizzie called from somewhere beyond the tall white blooms of the valerian plants.

"Mommy!"

"Hi! How was your day?"

"I ate all the stars!" Kylie exclaimed.

"You did?" came her mother's theatrical gasp.

"She means starflowers," Harper corrected in a long-suffering tone.

"How were they?" Lizzie asked then, in a grownup to grownup kind of voice.

"They were great," Juniper told her. Toni walked out to meet them, and Lizzie waved. Her little sister looked happy but tired, with dark circles under her eyes. Her flyaway blond curls were straining to escape the red bandana she wore.

Kylie pulled on Lizzie, vying for her attention. "We drew pictures and then—well, actually Juni drew pictures, and we colored them in—and then we played hide and seek in the garden, and I *won* because they couldn't find me ever until I started laughing and then–"

She kept chattering, but Toni's attention was diverted by another car rolling up through the redwoods that surrounded her home. Her stomach sank at the sight of her brother's truck. Every attempt that she and Juniper had made by call or by text to talk to him about extending her stay again had been shut down. He was determined to get Juniper back to Santa Cruz in time for school on Monday.

"Ethan!" Lizzie waved wildly as their brother stepped down from his truck. "You're early."

She went to greet him, holding Kylie under her arm like a sack of laundry that bounced and giggled as she walked.

"Come on, Harper." Juniper met Toni's eyes for a moment, then took her cousin's hand and turned toward the house. "Let's go get your stuff."

"Wait for me!" Kylie wriggled away from her mom and sprinted after the big girls.

Toni watched her go, stalling for time. Then she took a deep breath and walked toward her siblings. Her heart twisted as she got a good look at Ethan's face. The circles under his eyes had deepened, and he looked so much older than he was. He was only in his mid-thirties, but today he could have passed for Toni's older brother. Stress had taken its toll.

"Hey, Ethan." Toni put her arms around her little brother —well, her younger brother, who was about a foot taller than she was. He stood stiff and gave her an awkward pat on the back. "How are you?"

"I'm fine," he said shortly. "Just in a bit of a time crunch. I'm taking Juniper to my mom's house for lunch before we drive back down to Santa Cruz."

"Your mom's house?" Lizzie gave an exasperated snort and lightly shoved his arm. "What is wrong with you?"

"Nothing, what's wrong with *you*?" Ethan shot back, and Toni had a sudden vivid memory of them when they were as young as Lizzie's girls. The twins, Ethan and Emma, had always lived in a world of their own. That had left Lizzie, the youngest Flores, constantly vying for their attention. She had never much cared whether she was waiting on them or wrestling with them, so long as she was included. The oldest by a long shot and only related to the others through their father, Toni had always been more distant from the twins. But Lizzie had been her shadow on the days that she was home, and she had always admired her youngest sibling's verve.

"Saying 'my mom's house' to Toni as if it weren't her childhood home. As if it weren't her home *first*, in fact."

"For God's sake, Lizzie. I don't need you policing my word choice right now. None of us have lived there in decades."

"Oh? And so the six months that I spent in that cell block with my girls was what? A vacation?"

"An extended stay. And you're being ridiculous. It's not your house anymore. Or Toni's. Or mine. Why are we even—"

"My point is that you don't have to 'my mom' our sister. You could say 'Dad's house.' He lives there too, you know."

"Barely," Ethan muttered. Their father had finally retired from his career as a pilot a few years back, but he hadn't slowed down one iota. If anything, he spent even less time in Redwood Grove than before, and Toni couldn't blame him. If she shared a house with her stepmother, she wouldn't want to be home either. Actually, that was the primary reason that she had practically lived at Hoffman Farm growing up.

Ethan passed a hand over his eyes. "I don't have the energy for you right now, Liz."

Wordlessly, Lizzie put her arms around her brother. He stood stiff for a long moment and then wrapped an arm around her shoulders and leaned into her, resting his cheek on the top of her head for just a moment before straightening up again.

"Juniper!" he called. "Grab your stuff! Lizzie, go grab your gremlins so my daughter can pack."

Lizzie gave her big brother another shove and dropped a kiss on Toni's cheek. Then she turned and trotted toward the house. "Yo, womb fruit! Who wants waffles?"

"Waffles!" Kylie sprinted past her and yanked open the car door. Toni winced, half expecting the thing to fall off. The car had belonged to their dad for a solid twenty years before it was Lizzie's, and it was a small miracle that the thing was still in one piece.

"Harper!" Lizzie called up the porch steps. "Let's bounce!"

"I don't want to!" Harper's voice came from deep inside the house, barely audible.

"If we go now, we can hit the library before it closes."

Harper came out a moment later, dragging her backpack behind her. Juniper came out behind her and tossed Kylie's backpack down to Liz. She gave Ethan a nervous little wave.

"I want waffles!" Already in the car, Kylie stuck the top half of her body out the window and waved frantically at her mother and sister. "Hurry!"

"Okay, okay, we're out. Thanks for today." Lizzie pulled Toni into a tight hug as Harper ran to get in the car, and then they broke apart. Lizzie climbed into her car and disappeared down the drive. There was a long, awkward silence... and then Juniper walked toward her dad like she was marching to the gallows. Even so, Ethan's face softened as he reached out to hug his daughter.

"Hey, Juniper May. I missed you."

"I missed you too." Juniper returned the hug before stepping back and sucking in a steadying breath. "But I don't want to go back to Santa Cruz."

Ethan's brow furrowed. "Juniper, I'm not doing this again. Please. Let's just finish out the year, and this summer—"

Juniper pulled away from him. "I won't go."

Toni put a light hand on Ethan's arm and breathed a silent sigh of relief when he didn't shrug her off. "Come inside," she said softly. "I'll make some tea."

"You can't solve everything with tea, Antonia."

"You're right," she said lightly. "But taking a breather before saying things we might regret might help some."

"I'll make it," Juniper blurted eagerly before taking the porch steps two at a time.

"How are you really?" Toni asked once Juni was out of earshot.

"Oh, awesome. Yeah," Ethan muttered. "Just questioning every decision I've ever made in my life."

"That good, huh?"

"I thought if I stood by her..." he started, and then trailed off. When he spoke again, his voice was almost inaudible over the sound of the bees that surrounded them and the rush of the wind through the trees at the edge of the clearing. "I thought she'd be better by now. That she could've wrestled her demons. That she'd be there for Juniper through these years because I have no idea how to parent a teenage girl all on my own."

"You're not alone, Ethan. We're all here for you. Juniper has three aunts who adore her."

"And two supportive grandparents. I know. But you're all

here in Redwood Grove." He raked a hand through his hair and let out a groan. "I never should have moved her to a different county."

"It's not like you live in the North Pole, Ethan. Santa Cruz isn't that far."

"It's far enough. Too far for her to live here and still get to school every day. Unless you're volunteering to spend six hours in the car taking her back and forth twice a day."

"She doesn't want to go back to that school."

"Kids don't want to do a lot of things that are good for them," her brother shot back instantly. "They don't want to brush their teeth or eat vegetables, but that doesn't mean that you just let them do whatever they want."

"She's a great kid having a really tough time. Can't we offer her vegetables but also try to understand that, for whatever reason, she needs a different kind of nourishment right now? She's flourishing here, Ethan. I think she's where she's supposed to be. Not forever...just for right now."

Ethan shook his head and let out a snort. "It's easy being the fun aunt, isn't it? But it can't keep going like this. She needs guidance. I gave her more time, but she needs to come home now. Take her all summer if you want to."

"I'd be happy to. I love having her here. But she's dead set on not going back to school. She was broken when she got here. School isn't what she needs right now. Her friends in Santa Cruz aren't what she needs."

"And you're an expert on what she needs?"

"I know what it is to be a teenage girl without a mother," Toni said quietly. Ethan gave her a guarded glance and opened his mouth like he might argue with her, but then he snapped it shut again. "She needs me and Lizzie and Emma.

She needs meaningful work to occupy her hands and her mind and give her heart some peace."

Ethan stiffened his chin and glared at her. "What she needs to do is prepare to go to college."

"Does she? We didn't."

"That was a different time. A bachelor's degree is the new high school degree. She can't do a thing without it."

"She can literally do a million things without it." Toni's boots thumped with emphasis as she stomped up the steps to her place. "She can do whatever she sets her mind to. With or without spending the next month at a brick and mortar school. It won't make or break her. But I worry that making her leave now when she's finally found a little peace might."

Ethan followed her up the steps, but before he could reply, Juni called out.

"Hey guys," she said, opening the door and waving them in. "I made us some iced tea."

Ethan blinked and closed his mouth, opting to follow behind his daughter in silence as she led him inside. Toni followed close behind and watched carefully as Ethan took in the bundles of herbs that hung from the rafters, Toni's overflowing bookshelves, the view of the redwood trees out back. The air inside smelled like rosemary and lavender.

"Juniper, I know you like it here," he sighed. "But this isn't—"

"Hold that thought," Juniper interrupted. "Come sit down."

She led him over to the kitchen table, which was covered in neat stacks of papers. Ethan looked them over with suspicion and narrowed his eyes at Juniper.

"What's all this?"

"I've emailed my guidance counselor and each of my teachers about my current circumstances." Juniper sat down at the head of the table, her voice both bright and businesslike.

"You have, have you?" Ethan gave Toni a dark look.

"Don't give me the death stare!" Toni held her hands up and walked away. "I had nothing to do with any of this." She busied herself with bottling tinctures on the opposite side of the kitchen while Juniper passed her father a stack of papers.

"These are our emails back and forth. Given the trauma of Mom's return to rehab and the fact that I'm currently staying with family in Redwood Grove, they've agreed to let me finish out the school year early. I took all of the AP exams at the beginning of May, so I was basically just killing time in those classes anyway. My teachers agreed to let me turn in my final essays early, and I already have."

"But your attendance," Ethan protested weakly. "A total of thirty days and you'll be reported as truant. You've already missed close to that many."

"Once my grades for the year are locked in, we can circumvent the problem of attendance by officially withdrawing me from Santa Cruz High School and registering me as a homeschool student, since compulsory education laws in California extend to the age of eighteen." She pushed another printout in his direction.

"Homeschool," he said flatly.

"It's so easy in California, Dad." Her voice was less businesslike now, more pleading. "There are no real hoops to jump through. You just need to sign this paper saying that I'll be learning from home. Technically we'll be our own school."

She put another piece of paper in front of him, and he

read, "Redwood Grove Academy. Juniper, this doesn't seem—"

"I know, it's silly. You have to put a school name. That's just how the laws are set up. It's called a private school affidavit because the state of California treats each homeschooling family like a legal private school. It's all above board, Dad. I've done all of my research."

"I can see that, Juni. But—"

"I can't kill time indoors for another month, Dad. If I hear those school bells one more time, I'm gonna lose it. I mean, look at this place." Her voice rose slightly as she gestured toward the open door. "It's paradise. I'm learning things that actually matter. Nia could use my help, and Lizzie needs me. Let me stay, Dad. Please."

"And you won't be marked truant?" Ethan asked slowly as he scanned the papers. "Because the last thing I need is someone from CPS—"

"Talk to my guidance counselor if you want," Juniper said. "The school wants butts in seats even after AP tests because that's how they get their funding, but it's pointless. If you just fill out these forms, I can self-educate and graduate. Or go back to school next year, whatever. I can find out about the high school here if you want, see if their classes are worth going to. But that's in the fall. And honestly, I don't want to go to high school anymore."

"What about a diploma?"

"I can test for my GED whenever."

"And college?"

"If I decide to go to college, I can just get an associate's degree at Cabrillo and then transfer somewhere else. I'll learn more here than I will in school, Dad. You know I will."

Ethan leaned back in his chair and cast a look toward Toni, who quickly looked back to the little glass bottles she was filling with her rosemary tincture. Her brother let out a long, loud sigh.

"Okay, Juniper. I give. I'll sign your papers. But we revisit the issue at the end of summer. Deal?"

"Deal!" Juniper sprang up from her seat and threw her arms around Ethan's shoulders. "Thank you thank you thank you."

"I'm gonna miss you, kid."

Toni could hear the thickness in his voice, and it made her heart ache. This wasn't easy for her brother, and she hated that he was in pain.

"Maybe you should move home to Redwood Grove too," Juni said softly.

"I'll think about it," he said gruffly. "I have a lease and contracts and—"

"I know, Dad. But until then, we can still see each other. It's not that far. You can come visit."

"Will you come visit me, too?"

Juniper flinched visibly and settled back into her seat.

"What's wrong?" Ethan asked, flicking a glance between Toni and his daughter.

"I don't want to make you sad, Dad, but I...don't like being there. There's so many memories and..." She let out a shuddering breath. "It just hurts too much."

"Oh, Juniper." He stood and reached for his daughter, who rose and stepped into his arms for a bear hug. "I'm so sorry, kiddo."

Toni moved past them in silence, slipping out the side door as she blinked back tears. This was a painful situation all around. But in the end, staying here was best for Juni. She was sure of it. And who knew? Maybe his daughter's encouragement would be just the thing to bring Ethan back into the fold. If anyone could use some time in nature and some emotional support, it was her little brother.

Toni watched bees buzz around the tulsi, their saddlebags full of red pollen. The sun was warm on her face, drying her tears. Time to focus on gratitude. She had fantastic friends and an utterly magical place to live and work. And after living alone her whole adult life, she had her favorite kid in the world living with her through the summer, at least—maybe even longer. As for Juni, she was going to get some more time here in Redwood Grove to heal.

For Toni, that felt like the greatest gift of all.

20

Beth

BETH PACED the floor of the empty store, nervously watching the clock. She'd spent part of her day off and most of the morning getting everything pristine and ready for her first class at the shop. She had moved some center shelves to one side and set up a circle of folding chairs: one for her and five for the students who had signed up. There were extra chairs leaning up against the wall too, in case she got any walk-ins at the last minute. In her flyers and emails, she had encouraged them to show up early to buy the supplies they would need, but it was twenty minutes to the hour and still nary a student.

What if no one showed? It was a free class, after all. Easy to blow off at the last minute...

The bell chimed, and Beth turned to the door with a bright smile. She relaxed when she saw a familiar face instead of a new student, but her smile remained.

Juniper looked worlds better than she had the day that she and Beth had met. Her pale cheeks were infused with new color and a smattering of freckles. The bare ember of light in her eyes had been kindled into something bright and beautiful, and the smile that she gave Beth transformed her whole face.

"Hi!" Juniper pulled Beth into a hug. "How are you?"

"I'm well!" Beth said. "How are you?"

"I'm great. Guess why?"

Beth grinned. "Why?"

Juniper threw out her hands in celebration. "My dad finally agreed to let me finish out the school year early and stay in Redwood Grove! I'm loving my life right now."

"Congrats, that's awesome! Do you have a lot of friends here?" Beth asked.

"A lot of family. Three aunts, three cousins, two grandparents. And some other people who are nearly family. It got lonely in Santa Cruz, just me and my dad. I like having more of a tribe around, you know?"

"I get that," Beth said, trying not to let her smile falter. She was happy in Redwood Grove, and she loved her job and her little home above the shop, but she was still lonely here. Living all on her own was going to take some getting used to. Some days Beth wasn't sure she ever *would* get used to it. She missed her family in Maine like crazy.

"I've been spending most of my time with my Aunt Toni, working in her market garden and making herbal remedies. She's the coolest. You would love her. She's been all over the world, but she's super down to earth."

Beth smiled, thinking of her Aunt Anna. "I've got an aunt like that. She's a wildlife photographer."

Beth hadn't met her mother's half-sister until she was already an adult herself, but her long-lost aunt was as dear to her now as the family she had known her whole life.

"Super cool. Nia—that's what I call my aunt—she spent years working on farms all over the world. Europe, Australia, all over. She even ran a farm in Costa Rica for a while before she finally came home to Redwood Grove. I can't tell you how amazing it feels to plant seeds and make medicine after doing *nothing* in school for years."

Beth just smiled and nodded, touched by how alive and animated the teenage girl was.

"When I'm not with Nia, I'm watching my little cousins. Two little blondies, they're the cutest. My Aunt Lizzie is a single mom, so she really appreciates the help."

"And you have one more cousin in town?" Beth asked. "Closer to your age?"

"No, he's little too. I don't see him as much because his parents don't really need help, but they're gonna pay me to babysit him Saturday night so they can go out."

"Awesome," Beth said, willing herself not to look at the clock. Where were all of her students? "How's that colorwork sweater coming along?"

"Pretty slow," Juniper said with a shrug. "I've been busy. When I'm not working or babysitting, I've been reading my Aunt Nia's books. She has this whole personal library on herbalism and gardening and stuff. I'm learning tons, and then I actually get to put what I'm learning to work. That's the best part."

"Very cool."

The door opened then, and Beth jumped to attention. An

unfamiliar woman in her thirties walked in, and Juniper ran to meet her.

"Hi, Auntie Em!"

"I hate it when you call me that," the woman said, but she said it with a laugh and a hug. Juniper's aunt was a gorgeous woman with thick auburn hair and laugh lines around her eyes. She smiled at Beth over Juniper's shoulder and said, "Hi, I'm Emma. Juniper convinced me to come for your beginners class."

"Oh, hi!" Beth said. "Thank you! I mean, it's nice to meet you."

"She's my dad's twin," Juniper volunteered cheerfully. "Come on, Auntie Em, let's find you a really soft merino for your first scarf."

"What's merino?"

"It's a kind of wool," Juniper said, towing her aunt to a shelf full of multicolored hand-dyed yarn. "From a special kind of sheep? I think? Anyway, it's super soft and fun to work with. You don't want something stiff or plasticky. It hurts your fingers after a while."

"These colors are gorgeous," Emma said.

"Right?" Juniper chirped. "It's way more fun to knit something basic when the color keeps changing all on its own. What do you think of this green and gold one?"

The bell over the door chimed again, and Beth recognized one of the students who had signed up in person. She was a retired teacher who lived just outside of town, Beth recalled. She hurried to greet her and help her choose her first skein of yarn. Two more students walked in as Beth rang up the first purchase, and Juniper helped them choose their own skeins for the scarves they would be starting that day.

The final two students, a twelve-year-old girl and her mom, ran into the shop just as the class was set to start. They had already purchased their yarn the day that they had signed up, so they were all set.

One final student came sweeping in at the last minute, and Beth recognized the lady she had met on her first visit to Redwood Grove. Her cloud of snow-white hair and distinctive style were unforgettable.

"Room for one more?" asked Echo.

"Of course," Beth said, a rush of warmth rolling through her. This was even better than she could've hoped.

"Can you believe I've gone seventy years on this earth without learning to knit?" Echo asked with a smile and a shake of her head. "My grandmother and my mother both tried to teach me, but I was too flighty. I think I've finally settled down enough to pick it up, though. I'm told it's very soothing, and my old eyes are getting a bit tired for bracelet work. I need a new hobby."

"Come choose your yarn, Echo," Juniper called from across the store. "Let's find you something bright and beautiful."

"And soft," Echo said, crossing over to join her. "Nothing scratchy."

"Perish the thought!" Juniper exclaimed, and Echo laughed. "Check out these silk blends."

Beth couldn't have hoped for a better assistant.

Echo chose a hot-pink skein of chunky alpaca yarn, and Juniper helped her find the corresponding needle size. She even added two chairs to the circle while Beth was ringing up Echo's purchase, and then Beth hurried to join her students.

"Okay!" she said as she sat down. "Thank you for your patience, and welcome to our very first Intro to Knitting class! So there are a couple of things that we have to do before we get started. Myra," she said to the twelve-year-old, "will you show them your yarn?"

Grinning shyly, the girl held up the ball of pale blue yarn that she had chosen for her scarf.

"See how it's already wound?" Beth asked. "If you try to knit straight from the skeins you just bought, your yarn will get all tangled."

One of the students frowned and asked, "So we have to wind it first? By hand?"

"You could," Beth said with a grin, drawing out the word, "but that would take a while. It can be pretty tedious—and what's worse, it can be easy to make a mistake and end up with a tangled mess halfway through. Luckily for you, I have a solution." She hopped up and gestured to the yarn swift that sat on the front counter. "Any time you buy a skein of yarn, you're welcome to use our yarn swift. Come on over, and I'll show you how it works."

The handy spinning contraption made quick work of the skeins of yarn that hadn't been wound up yet, and then they returned to their seats to get started.

"Okay," Beth said, "so the first thing that we need to do is get the yarn onto the needles. That's called casting on, and it's the trickiest thing that we're going to learn tonight. Once you get that down, the actual knitting is easy. I want you to really get it, though, so we'll practice doing it a few times before we get to the knitting.

"There's more than one way to cast on, so I'll show you

my favorite method, and then I'll show you a couple of other ways, and you can see which one you like best."

Beth led them through it, with Juniper drifting around the circle and helping people when they faltered. Next they got into basic knit and purl stitches, and Beth's instruction gave way to general conversation as the students began to make headway with their projects. Beth was there to help them if they dropped a stitch, but other than that, they were already pretty self-sufficient.

"So," she told them at the end of the hour, "your homework assignment this week is to make your scarf as long as you like. If you went for a really wide scarf, you may want to come in for a second skein of yarn to get to a good length. Bring your project in and I'll show you how to add in that second ball of yarn. It's not hard. And then in our second class, I'll show you how to cast off! That's the term for getting the project off the needles without the whole thing unraveling on you. And once you've cast off on your scarves, we'll start knitting hats!"

"That was easier than I thought it would be," said the woman who had come in with her daughter. "Thank you so much."

"My pleasure," Beth said.

Juniper came up to hug her goodbye. "You're brilliant."

"*You're* brilliant," Beth told her. "Thanks for all of your help tonight."

"It was fun," Juniper said brightly. "I like being useful. Speaking of which, I've gotta run. I'm babysitting Lizzie's girls tonight."

As everyone else cleared out, Echo stayed right where she

was and kept on knitting—even as Beth cleared the chairs away and moved the shop's center shelves back into place. Eventually she held up her five-inch scarf and looked at Beth with shining eyes.

"I can't believe it took me seventy years to learn how to do this."

Beth grinned. "It's fun, isn't it?"

"It's extraordinary. But then, every act of transformation is extraordinary in its own way." She tucked the work in progress carefully into her bag and turned her shining eyes back to Beth. "How are you adjusting to your new life, dear one?"

Beth spread her hands and shrugged. "Slowly? Tonight was fun."

"It *was* fun, wasn't it?" Echo stood and folded her chair, putting it in line with its fellows. "Thank you for that. I look forward to many more classes to come."

"I'm glad you came."

"So am I." Echo smiled fondly at Beth and pulled her into a hug. "You're a marvelous young woman."

"Thanks," Beth said. "You too."

Echo laughed with a sound like wind chimes. "Good night, dear heart."

"Good night."

Beth set about closing out the register, but it was only a couple of minutes before the bell above the door sounded again. They were technically closed, but she hadn't locked up yet.

"Did you forget something, Echo?" Beth asked without looking up, in the middle of counting the cash in the register.

When there was no answer, Beth paused her count and turned to the door... and nearly fainted dead away at the sight of her ex-boyfriend.

"Hi, Beth," Josh said with that same bashful smile that had charmed her four years earlier. "Do you have a minute?"

21

AVA WAS TOO busy with the looming launch of the Redwood
Café to spend much time with Nolan during daylight hours,
but he was always there on the periphery. While she worked
to prepare for the grand reopening, Nolan did everything
else. He ran the farm, drove soup and visitors to Gran, took
care of Phoenix, and made all the changes to the house that
Marisol had suggested for Gran's return home.

And then most evenings, when Ava was still plugging
away at the café with flagging energy, he came along and
spirited her away. They drove down to Santa Cruz or up to
Half Moon Bay, enjoying the ride as much as the restaurants.
If Ava could keep her eyes open long enough, they enjoyed a
movie at their own private drive-in before she retired to her
childhood room, feeling all of fifteen again.

It was a strange balance, being the matriarch during the

day and a lovestruck fool at night. But after a long day of interviews and paperwork and bills, it felt so good to surrender to Nolan's plans for the evening: sunsets, leisurely dinners, nostalgic movies.

It hadn't been long at all, but already her life in San Diego was starting to feel like a distant memory. Like an alternate reality she wasn't entirely sure she wanted to return to. Sure, she texted her son most days and kept in touch with her friends there, but more and more, this place was feeling like–

"Avalon!" Lyra's voice snapped Ava out of her ruminations. She had been staring at a long list of restaurant supplies without really seeing them.

"Hey, Mom," she sighed, reluctant to engage. Her mother's shining eyes and overbright smile made Ava's stomach clench. A manic-looking Lyra was never a good thing.

"You've been working nonstop since I got here. I've barely seen you. Let me take you out to lunch."

The defensive wall in Ava's chest crumbled just a bit. It was true that she and her mother had spent hardly any time together, despite the fact that they were sleeping in the same house. Ava was up at dawn most days, while her mother rarely emerged from her room before noon. Not that she slept that late—Ava could smell Lyra's coffeemaker going around nine and heard her chatting with friends shortly thereafter— but it was close to noon by the time she came downstairs for food. They each visited Gran, but generally went on alternating days. Lyra had invited Ava to ride in her convertible more than once, but Ava had always begged off, saying that she had to conduct interviews for café staff, which was mostly true. But she had to admit that part of the reason she was staying so busy was to avoid her mother.

The less time she spent with her, the less Lyra could disappoint her.

"Aren't you hungry?" Lyra pressed when Ava didn't answer right away.

"Yeah," Ava conceded as her stomach growled. "I guess I am."

"Just into town and back," Lyra said. "It won't take long. And it's on me."

"Okay." Ava stood and stretched. "Thank you."

"Please." Lyra waved her thanks away and headed for the door. "It's not often you let me do anything for you, and you've been working so hard. It's my pleasure."

Ava paused on her way out the door and knelt to pat Phoenix's head. His thick golden tail thumped on the ground, and he rolled to one side, inviting belly rubs. Ava obliged, carefully avoiding his cracked ribs. He was still a ways away from being able to run and jump, but he was hobbling up and down the ramp just fine.

"I can't wait to get Gran home," she murmured, scratching Phoenix behind his ears. "You two invalids can recuperate together. You'll like that, won't you? You can keep her company."

Phoenix's tail sped up. His brown eyes were simultaneously happy and soulful, and Ava could almost believe that he understood her.

"Ahem." Lyra cleared her throat. Ava looked up to where her mother stood by the back door. Was it just her imagination, or was there a brittle edge to Lyra's smile? "Shall we?"

"Yeah." Ava rose to her feet. "Sorry."

"Oh, I don't mind." Lyra's voice matched her expression. Manic for sure.

Ava never knew what to make of her mother's moods. When she was young, Lyra had been intense and changeable, screeching at her one minute and smothering her with kisses the next. Then Lyra had started to leave for longer and longer spans of time. When she was back on the farm, it usually felt to Ava like there was a pane of glass between them. Her mother was bright and beautiful, showering her with attention and gifts that she had gathered while she was away. But she was also always... not fully there. Not like Gran.

Ava pushed those thoughts aside as she sank into her mom's convertible. She was a grown woman, and those hazy childhood memories were ancient history. They were just two adults now, getting on the best they could. Maybe if she spent more time with her mother, it would be easier to relate to her as a real person and not just as a figment of her childhood memories.

"Redwood House?" Lyra asked in a chipper voice. "I am absolutely addicted to their eggs Benedict."

"Sounds good," Ava agreed, pulling the seatbelt across her chest. She unbuckled it a moment later when Lyra drove to the back gate and looked at her expectantly.

"Thanks, doll," Lyra said when Ava closed the gate behind them and got back into the car.

"I really need to get an automatic gate installed ASAP. Most of the café traffic will come from the One, but it would be nice to give the locals an easy way in."

Lyra replied with a thoughtful *hmm* that may or may not have been an agreement. Behind her movie star sunglasses, her eyes were fixed on the windy mountain road. Ava turned the radio on and scanned through fuzzy channels until she found the Golden Oldies station. As she turned up the volume on a familiar old song, a slow smile appeared on her mother's face. Lyra hummed under her breath, half dancing in her seat as she drove, and Ava felt a reluctant smile overtake her own face.

Gran had been the center of Ava's childhood, the ground under her feet and the gravity that held her to it. But she had plenty of vivid memories of Lyra too. And in most of them – most of the good ones, at least – her mother was dancing. When Ava was still small and light, Lyra used to spin her all around the kitchen until she shrieked with laughter. Even when she was taller, Lyra would invite her to stand on her pristine cowboy boots and slow dance around the dinner table.

"We're early," Lyra murmured when she parked in front of the Redwood House restaurant. She lifted her shades and peered up the stairs into the shade of the restaurant.

"Early for what?" Ava asked. Lyra gave her a quick, startled look that brought her apple-sized lenses back down over her bright blue eyes. When she spoke, already halfway out of the convertible, her tone was light.

"For lunch. I wanted a salad, not eggs. Looks like we've got about twenty minutes to kill?"

"You said you wanted Eggs Benedict–" Ava started, but Lyra cut her off.

"I said I'm addicted to it. But I feel like a Caesar salad with salmon." Lyra's gaze drifted across the street, and her white teeth flashed in a sudden grin. She grabbed Ava's hand. "Come with me, Avalon. We're going shopping." She laughed at Ava's low groan and towed her across the street to a newish shop that Ava had seen in passing but never set foot in. "Stop being such a stick in the mud. You gotta live a little, kid."

"Shopping isn't my idea of fun," Ava protested in a hushed voice as her mother opened the store's glass door.

"Then let *me* have some fun by buying you some new clothes," Lyra insisted.

Ava bit back a sigh and smiled politely at the woman behind the checkout counter. The truth was, she could use a couple new things. She had been frenzied and fearful when she'd thrown some clothes in a bag weeks before, thinking only of getting to the hospital. As a result, she'd been washing her clothes twice a week, and some of her older shirts were coming out of the dryer with new holes. She'd mended a couple, but others were too threadbare to bother.

What she needed were comfortable clothes for the house and the hospital, sturdy clothes for the farm, and something decently presentable for the café's grand reopening. But the dress that pulled her to the back of the store was none of the above. It was sleeveless with light, gauzy fabric that was the exact color of the ocean on a bright summer day.

"That dress was *made* for you, Avalon," Lyra gushed. "Try it on."

Ava didn't even argue. She draped the dress over her arm, picked up a few everyday shirts, and headed for the changing room, feeling just a little giddy. Behind the closed door, she tried the shirts on first. They were printed with local artwork, which she loved. They were also light and comfortable, and the nicer blouse was still practical enough to withstand any kitchen mishaps that might befall her on opening day.

Once she'd put the shirts into a neat little pile, she slipped the blue dress over her head, heart fluttering as she faced the mirror.

It was a perfect fit. And even in the dim light of the changing room, it had her eyes shining a more vivid shade of blue than she could remember seeing in a long time. She looked...

Happy.

"If you keep me waiting one more minute," Lyra threatened in a light voice, "I'm going to bang that door down."

"It's a curtain," Ava corrected with a chuckle.

"So I'll have no trouble making good on my threat."

She shook her head and pushed the curtain aside. Lyra stood stock still for a moment, and then she put one hand over her heart.

"You look absolutely beautiful. I'm buying it for you."

Ava smiled and shook her head. "I can buy it for myself. I'm getting a few shirts, too."

"So long as the dress goes home with you, I'm satisfied. But I'm buying lunch," Lyra added in a threatening tone. "No arguing on that."

"Fine. Whatever you say, Mom."

Ava pulled the curtain closed again and smiled into the mirror one last time. She wondered what Nolan would think of her new dress... even as she tried not to wonder when that had started to matter so much.

Forty minutes later, she and her mother were halfway through their yummy salads when a woman Lyra's age rushed up to them in a flurry of greeting. Her dye-red hair was cut shoulder length and meticulously curled. A cloud of perfume arrived at their table a second after she did, and Ava tried unsuccessfully to hold back a coughing fit.

"I'm so sorry. I hope you haven't been waiting too long." The woman sat down next to Ava, whose throat burned with the chemical scent of her perfume. She wanted to ask *Waiting for what?* But she was afraid to open her mouth.

She scooted her chair toward the balcony railing, trying to catch the fresh air that blew by just beyond their table.

"We were just enjoying a girls' day out," Lyra said with a breezy smile. "Belinda, this is my daughter, Avalon. Avalon, this is Belinda."

"She is just your spitting image."

"Isn't she gorgeous?" Lyra asked, beaming.

"It is so lovely to finally meet you, Avalon." Belinda pulled a folder from her bag and slapped it on the table, brows raised. "So I thought we could start off by looking at some comp properties for the area."

"Some what?" Ava looked between her mother and Belinda in confusion.

She opened the folder to reveal a printout of a real estate listing. "This place here is the most similar and currently in escrow for a pretty penny, as you can see. A bit more square footage, but your mother's place has more property and has been updated more recently."

Ava stared at the sprawling whitewashed home, struck dumb.

Oblivious to her reaction, Belinda flipped to the next listing. "Now this one closed late last year, but they probably could have gotten another hundred K if they had waited until summer. This is the perfect time to put a property like yours on the market."

Ava blinked hard and turned toward her mother. Lyra was hyper-fixated on Belinda, but there was no doubt she knew Ava was looking at her. A muscle at the corner of her smiling lips had begun to twitch.

"What do you think you're doing, Lyra?" Ava managed under her breath.

Lyra reached for her now icy hand and gave it a squeeze. "Sweetheart, I know you don't want to hear it, but we really do have to consider all of our options here."

"No." Ava pulled back, shaking her head furiously. "Absolutely not. Gran isn't selling the farm."

Lyra's eyes narrowed in a warning glare, but her mouth stayed frozen in that forced, perma-grin. "Your grandmother will be in a wheelchair for the rest of her life. Do you really think that the *farm* is the best place for her?"

"It's the *only* place for her," Ava shot back, not bothering to whisper now. If her mother didn't want to air their dirty laundry in front of a near stranger, she shouldn't have ambushed her like this.

Lyra took a deep breath and shot an apologetic grimace toward the realtor, like she was having trouble staying patient with her hard-headed daughter. She fished into her purse and pulled out a crumpled brochure for an assisted living facility in San Jose.

"Nope," Ava snapped. "Not happening. Not on my watch."

"Avalon, your grandmother needs daily care. She needs *professional* care."

"Marisol is going to be there. She's a nurse," Ava protested. "And I can help."

"Marisol *used* to be a nurse," Lyra said primly. "And you have a life to get back to. Your own home and family."

Ava just shook her head, speechless. Gran was family. And sure, she had responsibilities in San Diego, but she would figure it out...

Next to her, Belinda sat frozen and wide-eyed, clearly baffled by this unexpected confrontation. She must have sensed her commission ebbing away, because after a moment of silence, she threw herself into the fray.

"Actually, my great aunt has been at Morrey Pines for five years." Belinda opened the brochure and pointed to a smiling lady with a purple perm. "That's her there. She *loves* her apartment."

"Gran doesn't *want* to live in an apartment," Ava hissed with quiet rage. "She wants to come home!"

Belinda gave her a condescending smile. "Sweetheart, there comes a time that we have to do what's best for our elders. And it's not always what they want. They're like children in that way. They can't fully understand what's good for them anymore."

Ava squeezed her eyes shut and shook her head. This wasn't happening. God, this was so typical of her mother. Her kindness always came with strings, some unexpected trap that snapped shut at the last second.

And who was the fool who kept falling for it?

"Ava!" Her eyes flew open at the sound of Nolan's voice. He was walking toward them along the center aisle of the wraparound porch, carefully navigating chairs as he hauled a heavy crate of produce toward the kitchen door. "I didn't–"

His eyes caught on the papers in front of her, and Ava's stomach dropped as she watched the expression on Nolan's face shift from something bright and beautiful to a look of devastated betrayal.

"Nolan, wait," she called as he strode away.

He pushed the kitchen door open with his knee and disappeared.

Dang it.

She wriggled to push her chair back, but she was pinned between the railing and the realtor seated beside her.

"Excuse me, Belinda, can you let me out please?"

"Certainly. Is everything all right?" Belinda asked, gathering the papers and tapping them back into a neat pile instead of moving.

Ava's heart beat like a drum as she shoved the table back with a screech. "I just need to-"

"Avalon! Stop that right now and focus. We're not done here." Lyra snatched the printouts of the multi-million-dollar properties back from a bewildered Belinda.

"You might not be done, but I definitely am." She turned to Belinda and said in a much firmer tone, "Move, please."

The real estate agent flicked an anxious glance between her and her mother, clearly between a rock and a hard place.

"Um, I'm not sure exactly what's happening, but—"

"Nolan!" Ava shouted as he appeared again, his long legs making short work of the floorboards. "Wait!"

He didn't even look at her—just disappeared down the back steps that led from the porch to the parking lot. With a muttered curse, she grabbed her purse and shopping bag, ducked under the table, crawled past her mother's legs, and rose up.

"Avalon!" Lyra sounded scandalized. "What in the world do you think you're doing? Belinda has graciously given up her lunch hour to meet with us on short notice, and you're being unbearably rude."

Ava ignored her. "We won't be selling," she told Belinda. "Sorry to waste your time."

Then she took off toward the parking lot. But by the time she got there, Nolan's truck was already halfway down the street. She cursed again and scanned the parking lot that the Redwood House shared with Wild Roots, desperate for a ride. No amount of money could entice her back into her mother's convertible.

The automatic front doors of Wild Roots slid open, revealing a small grocery cart brimming with produce and beeswax candles. The owner brightened when she saw Ava. She tossed her fluffy white hair over one shoulder and gave the younger woman a small, regal wave.

Ava had never been so happy to see someone.

"Echo!" Ava ran across the parking lot and plucked the canvas grocery bags from the cart. "Could you give me a ride home?"

Behind her, Lyra shouted something from the restaurant porch. Echo glanced at her, then looked back at Ava with a conspiratorial smile.

"Sure thing, sugarplum." She opened the trunk of her aged Cadillac, and Ava deposited the groceries. "Hop in."

Echo was unusually quiet on the drive to the farm, humming along with the radio as she navigated the winding mountain road. Probably for the best, since Ava's brain was firing on all cylinders.

What must Nolan think of her right now?

When they pulled up alongside the farm's back gate, Echo leaned over to kiss Ava's cheek.

"I've gotta get home before my mochi melts."

"Thanks for the ride, Echo."

"Anytime, sweetheart. When's your gran coming home?"

"The doctor said she should be cleared to leave next week."

"Glad to hear it." Echo squeezed Ava's arm as she opened the car door. "It's good to have you back."

Ava shot a weak smile at the older woman and nodded.

She had just been thinking that herself. Only now, Lyra had thrown a wrench in the works like she always did, sending the freshly well-oiled machine of her life to a screeching halt.

Only this time, Ava wasn't going to stand for it. This time, she was going to put her foot down and stand firm. She'd not only found a purpose here in Redwood Grove. She'd also been granted bonus time with her beloved Gran and had rekindled her romance with her first love. Sure, there were things that needed to be worked out, but she was more content now than she'd ever been.

And she'd be damned if she let Lyra take that away from her.

22

Beth

"WHAT ARE YOU DOING HERE, JOSH?"

"You said that you got a job at a knitting store in Redwood Grove." He walked across the store until he was just across the counter from where Beth stood frozen at the register. "It wasn't hard to find."

"I didn't ask *how*—" Beth cut herself off with a huff. "Just a minute." She finished counting the day's cash, returned it to the register, and locked the drawer.

"I wasn't sure I would get here before the place closed," Josh said.

"You didn't." Beth made herself look at him, and her stomach flip-flopped. Looking at him *hurt*. He was the only boyfriend she'd ever had. She had moved across the country for him. And he had broken her heart. "Why are you here?"

"I wanted to see you."

"*Why?*" she asked again.

"I miss you," he said simply. The look on his face was sincere, but Beth didn't feel any of the relief or elation that she had imagined feeling when, in the early days after their breakup, she had imagined Josh crawling back with apologies. She just felt... *frustrated.* Today had been such a good day. A *great* day. She had taught her first class ever, and it couldn't have gone better. And now Josh had to come in uninvited and make it all about him?

Why couldn't he just let her move on?

Some of what Beth was feeling must have shown on her face because the little bit of hope on Josh's face broke into something else, into guilt and a grief that surprised her.

"I know that the way I treated you was... not, like, unforgivable, but definitely not cool. That cross-country drive was so stressful, and all I could think about was the new job and how I shouldn't have let you come with me, how I just needed to focus on work and getting established in this whole new state–"

"You came all the way here to tell me that?" Beth asked flatly.

"I came to tell you that I made a mistake." Josh reached across the counter to take Beth's hand, but she pulled away. He gave her a pleading look and said, "Let me buy you dinner. No pressure, I just want to talk. Please."

Beth's shoulders slumped.

Despite how he'd ended things, he wasn't a terrible guy. And he *had* made the long drive down.

Plus, she was starving. "Fine."

Josh responded with a brilliant smile, and Beth felt another wave of overwhelming, conflicting emotions wash over her. She loved that smile, but she was so hurt and angry at the way he'd treated her.

"You'll feel better once you eat," he assured her. "You're just hangry."

"I'm not *just* anything, Josh," Beth muttered even as she followed him out the door. "You dumped me immediately after letting me follow you across the country."

"I did," he agreed solemnly. Then he smirked at her. "*And* you're hangry."

Beth had to fight back a smile, because he wasn't wrong. Her intro to knitting class had gone right through dinner, and she had been too nervous to eat beforehand. But she wouldn't give him the satisfaction of agreeing with him. She just turned away and locked up the shop.

"How's this place?" Josh asked, gesturing to the restaurant across the way.

"It's good." Beth studied her ex-boyfriend in the last of the day's light. Josh's hair was a little longer now, long enough to brush the tops of his shoulders. And God, his face was so beautiful. Maybe a tiny bit leaner than it had been when Beth was cooking for him every night... She hadn't noticed that when she was going through all his latest photos on social media. Which, Beth realized as they made their way across the street, she hadn't done in quite a while now. Dang, she'd been doing well. Why did he have to barrel in and ruin the progress she had made?

"Hey Beth!" the hostess greeted her as they walked up the stairs. Beth hadn't been in Redwood Grove very long, but she was already pretty much a regular at the one little restaurant that was open every day for breakfast, lunch, and dinner. It was so much easier to walk across the street than it was to go upstairs and cook herself a meal for one.

"Hey, Marcie," Beth greeted her.

"Table for two?"

"Yes please."

She led them to a table on the deck that overlooked a steep drop in the hillside and put them shoulder to shoulder with a few of the redwood trees that gave the town its name. Beth already knew what she wanted, so she just looked out through the trees as Josh perused the menu. Golden sunbeams slanted across the mountains, casting the evergreen forest in a fiery light that made Beth think of Maine in the fall.

"Hey, Beth!" Lizzie waggled her eyebrows at Beth as she walked over. They'd met a few times before, and the woman looked surprised to see her accompanied by a guy rather than the book she'd buried her nose in on each of the other occasions. She paused just behind Josh, who was still frowning at his menu, and tilted her head to one side.

"Good to see you." Beth greeted her with a smile and a slight shake of her head. *Nope, nothing to get excited about.* "Hey, any chance you're the Aunt Lizzie that Juniper was telling me about?"

"One and the same," Lizzie confirmed. "Small town, huh?"

"I'm used to it," Beth said. "I'm from small-town Maine. Honestly, I love it."

"Me too. Wouldn't want to live anywhere else. I was able to pick up enough shifts to get caught up on rent, and my girls couldn't be happier to spend time with their big cousin."

"I love that."

"Family," Lizzie said with a happy sigh. "So what can I get you?"

"I'll have the bison meatballs with polenta, please."

"Sure thing. Anything to drink?"

"What specials do you have today?" Beth asked.

"We've still got the blackberry thyme, and they just made a Meyer lemon and strawberry blend."

"Oh, I'll try that one. Please."

"Done and done." Lizzie turned to Josh. "And for you?"

"I'll take the burger. Well done."

"Cheese on that?"

"No. And no pickles."

"Anything to drink?"

"I'll try the local IPA."

"Coming right up," Lizzie said.

"Thank you," Beth called as she walked away. When she looked back at Josh, he was watching her with a bemused smile. "What?"

"I forgot how you are with, like, waitstaff and stuff."

Beth blinked at him. "What are you talking about?"

"Like they're your friends, or like you might just flip it around and start waiting on them. It's cute."

"I like coming here, and she's really nice." Beth looked away, trying to enjoy the dramatic golden-shadow contrast of the forest at dusk. She was wishing that she hadn't agreed to dinner with Josh.

"Sure. Yeah."

Beth was quiet until Lizzie came back with their drinks, and she downed half of her strawberry shrub in one go. Man, that was good. Their cocktails were probably fabulous, though Beth had yet to try one. She'd never been much of a drinker. It would be fun to get her Aunt Gayle out for a visit, though. She and Mom would love this place.

"You like your drink?" Josh asked, just to have something to say.

"Yeah, it's good. Yours?"

He shrugged. "It's okay."

"How are things in Half Moon Bay?" Beth asked as they waited for their food.

"I'm not staying."

Beth was startled into silence for a moment.

"What do you mean?" she asked at last.

"I got a job in San Francisco. Well, actually my dude Cory from high school got me a job at his startup. Remember him? He came to visit a couple times when he was home from Berkeley."

"Sure, I remember Cory. But what about your job in Half Moon Bay? Your lease on the apartment?" She'd left only weeks before, and literally everything had changed for him?

Josh shrugged. "Quit the job, got out of the lease. It wasn't cheap, but I managed it. This job in the city pays *twice* as much as the one in Half Moon Bay did, Beth. And that wasn't chump change to begin with."

Beth nodded dumbly. She managed a smile for Lizzie as the server set their food down.

Happy for something to do with her hands, she dug into her meal. The polenta was crazy delicious, rich and decadent without being soupy or dry. And the meatballs were just phenomenal, as good as anything that her mom made. And *that* was saying something. She couldn't wait to bring her here when she came to visit.

"I think you'd really like it, Beth."

At her name, she started and looked up. "Like what?"

"San Francisco," Josh said, half laughing. "What else?"

"I'm not big on big cities," Beth said, scraping the last of the polenta from her plate. So strange she had to say that out loud. Surely, he should know by now how much she loved getting lost in the magic of the forest...pushing herself on an amazing hike.

"But big cities have the best food," he pressed, leaning closer. "You'd go crazy for the restaurants there. There's this one that requires a reservation six months in advance. They have a twelve-course tasting menu that costs five hundred bucks."

She just shrugged, suddenly wondering how much longer she had to sit here and listen to him. A small shockwave went through her chest as she realized how eager she was to get away from the person she had spent weeks pining for. He hadn't asked her a single question about her life here, or what it had been like to start over from scratch. Alone. Thousands of miles from family.

If this were their first date, it would have been a hard pass. And, dang, was that realization freeing.

Lizzie popped her head outside and shot her a questioning look. Beth nodded. Yup. She was more than ready for the check.

Josh's hand shot out and clutched at hers. "Come back with me tonight."

Beth looked him in the eye, sure that she had heard him wrong. "What?"

"We'll go to my new favorite bar, and then to this amazing breakfast place in the morning. Chillax for a few days. Reconnect." He waggled his eyebrows, and Beth almost gagged.

"That's a really weird ask, Josh. On, like, so many levels. First off, I have work tomorrow."

"Oh." He deflated a bit. "Right. Of course. That's fine."

She just stared at him. What was this guy doing?

"You could drive up on your next day off," Josh said, perking up again.

"What are you..." Beth trailed off, shaking her head.

"Look, I made a mistake," Josh said with quiet urgency as he gripped her hand tighter. "I made such a mistake, letting you go. I'll be straight with you. I've been dating. And being single might *sound* like fun–"

"That does not sound like fun," she muttered.

"But it's such a drag, Beth. It just made me realize how much I miss you. Always having somebody there at the end of the day. Things were so easy with you. And I thought that I didn't want that, but... now that you're not there, I can see how amazing it was. You know what I mean?"

Beth was saved from answering by Lizzie, who came up to their table with a big smile.

"Thank you so much for coming," Lizzie said, dropping the check on the table. "Good to see you again, Beth."

"I'll get that," Josh said as Beth tugged her hand free and reached for the check. He handed Lizzie his credit card without taking his eyes off of Beth. The server headed off as Josh tried to take her hand again. "So like I was saying, I want us to get back together. I know there are things we need to talk through. We both have some work to do, some annoying tendencies and stuff, but I know we can make it work. I don't suppose there's anything in this town open past eight where we can hang and chat? Or did you want to show me your new place?"

"I do not, no," Beth replied.

Josh rocked back a couple of inches, nonplussed. "You don't what?"

"I don't want to show you my new place."

"Oh." His smile faltered. "Okay. Maybe next weekend you can come—"

"And I don't want to visit you. Or move to San Francisco." Beth spoke gently, but she made sure that her words didn't leave any room for uncertainty.

That didn't stop him from asking again, though.

"Seriously? You don't want to get back together?"

"Correct." She almost laughed but just barely managed to keep a straight face. "I definitely do not want to get back together."

"Wow." He slumped back in his chair. "Okay. I didn't expect..." He cleared his throat and shrugged. "Yeah, I guess I'm just surprised, is all."

Beth bit back a smile. "Sometimes people surprise each other."

Weird. She would've expected to feel angry or some sense of vengeance after the way he'd surprised her with their breakup. Instead, all she felt was relief. She'd dodged the proverbial bullet by not hitching her wagon to his permanently.

"Thanks for dinner, Josh. It was good to see you." Beth stood, and Josh looked up at her with a pained facsimile of a smile.

"Was it?"

"It was. I think I needed this. It was good to get some

closure." She had fallen head over heels for his good looks and fun vibe at nineteen, but in reality, she wanted something deeper.

Some*one* deeper.

She only wished she'd realized it sooner.

"Closure," he repeated.

"Yeah. Good night, Josh. Congrats on the new job."

"Thanks," he said after a beat. "See you around, I guess."

She walked away, thinking that his suggestion about "chillaxing" actually sounded pretty good. But she would do it alone, in her wonderful little home, with a Jane Austen movie and none of the snarky comments that Josh made whenever they watched anything even slightly romantic. So maybe she felt a little lonely once in a while. She was still pretty new to town, and that would change. At least she was free to do whatever the heck she wanted, in the company of someone she really quite liked.

Herself.

She glided down the wooden steps of the restaurant, feeling lighter than she had in a long time.

23

Ava

Ava had called his number multiple times and then searched the whole farm for Nolan's truck, but it was nowhere to be found. So she walked back up to the main house and slouched into one of the porch chairs, folding her arms over her chest to warm the block of ice sitting dead center.

Of course he hadn't headed straight home. He was probably right in the middle of his deliveries for the day. What had she been thinking, running after him like some lovesick teenager, anyway? Sure, he was angry. And rightfully so. If she'd seen what he'd seen, she'd likely have jumped to conclusions, too. It was her reaction to seeing him walk away that was killing her right now.

She felt empty.

Bereft.

And that was ridiculous. They'd only just reconnected. And it wasn't like they'd promised each other forever or something. She had a whole life in San Diego. She had a son she'd left behind to come up here and take care of Gran. As soon as she was home and the café was up and running, Ava would be heading back for Ryan's high school graduation.

And then what?

She rose to her feet and walked across the yard to the café. Inside, she stood still for a minute and let herself admire the progress they had made in such a short time. She and Greta and Marisol had scrubbed every inch of the building until it shone. Nolan had sanded down the old, peeling furniture and painted the chairs and tables red and blue and purple using half-full cans of paint that a friend had given him. One wall held old black-and-white photos of Hoffman Farm and Redwood Grove. Another was covered with vibrant abstract paintings so full of movement and color that they took Ava's breath away. Greta had shyly offered them up, and Ava had been astounded to learn that the quiet, willowy girl had painted them herself.

The restaurant was stocked. The staff was hired. Marisol was ready to spearhead Gran's recovery, and Nolan had the farm in hand. As soon as Ava found a general manager for the café, she could walk away with a clean conscience, despite what her mother said.

But is that really what you want? asked a voice in the back of her mind.

Ava's phone buzzed in her pocket, and she pulled it out, sure it was Nolan. She was surprised to see Ryan's name, and a tiny jolt of fear pierced her gut. She and her son texted back and forth most days, but he wasn't big on calling.

"Hey, kid," she answered.

"Hey, Mom," Ryan said. There was no panic in his voice, but Ava could hear an edge of... something. Worry? Anxiety?

"What's up?" she asked, trying to keep her tone light.

"Maggie said I should call you."

"Oh?"

"She said you're still planning to come down for graduation."

"Of course."

Ryan paused. "Mom, I'm not going to be at graduation."

"What? You're not graduating?" Ava felt an anxious edge creep into her tone, but she couldn't help it.

"Of course I'm graduating," Ryan said, exasperated. "I'm just not going to walk. I told you that."

Ava was quiet as she searched her memory, nearly certain that her son hadn't said anything of the sort. He had grumbled about it, yes, calling the ceremony overblown and pointless. But he had never outright said that he wouldn't participate.

"I've decided..." Her son took a deep breath and let it out in a rush. "Mom, I'm going to enlist on my birthday," he continued. His tone was quiet, almost frightened. Did he actually care how she was going to react? Ava had thought that she had lost any sway she had over her son a long time ago. And she had, she decided a second later. Her reaction wouldn't change anything. That didn't mean that she didn't have the power to hurt his feelings, guarded though they might be.

"On your birthday," she repeated quietly, buying herself time. It wasn't a total shock. He'd talked about it before, and she'd come to grips with the fact that he might actually do it—mostly. But so soon? Five days before graduation.

Dear God, he was barely a man...

"Yeah." His voice brightened with excitement. "Boot camp doesn't start for a few weeks, so Eli and I are going to leave as soon as I enlist. We're going to take his car and road trip as far as we can before then. Mags said she's gonna try to make Gran's party. I figured we could stop in on our way up the coast."

A peace offering, Ava recognized. A quick family visit before his life was no longer his own.

She'd take it.

"We'd love to see you," Ava told her son.

His sigh of relief melted her heart. It made her think of the little towheaded boy that he'd been when she was still the center of his world. Letting go of her children was the hardest thing she'd ever done, but Ryan had been pulling away for so long that the pain had been spread out over years instead of hitting her in a sudden blow the way it had when she dropped Maggie off at college.

The sound of a bell ringing in the distance echoed over the phone, interrupting her bittersweet musings.

"Mom, I gotta go. I've got to get to my last class. Text me the date of Gran's party, and I'll make sure we're there in time."

"I'm looking forward to it," she said, blinking back a stinging rush of tears.

It would be all right. Her son was smart, resilient, and stubborn. He'd find his way.

The phone disconnected, and Ava tucked it back into her pocket, determined to focus on the positive. Her son was coming to visit. It had been a long time since she and Gran and the kids had all been in the same place at the same time. Surely that would do them all some good.

She had to admit, the sudden call felt a little like kismet or fate. Up until this minute, she had been in denial that her son was grown. That he actually didn't need her anymore. At least, not in the way he used to. He'd always been pretty independent, but the past couple of years, it had been so evident that he couldn't wait to fly the coop. And what was a coop without chickens?

Nothing but an empty pile of wood and nails.

Nothing compared to what she had here in Redwood Grove. The sister she had in Toni. The purpose she had found in reinvigorating the café. The privilege of spending Gran's final years here, with her, on the farm they both loved.

And Nolan... San Diego had nothing on him.

When Ava finished the odd jobs that she had set herself to in the café, she walked back over to the farmhouse. Lyra's car was nowhere to be seen, and she wondered how long her mother would stay away, sulking. She hoped long enough for her to have a chance to talk with Nolan.

She headed inside and grabbed the bag full of new clothes, then carried them upstairs to her room. When she passed her mother's room, she paused and then did a double-take, her stomach clenching.

Empty. No suitcases or clothes strewn about the floor. Just the unmade bed and a dirty coffee cup on the nightstand.

Lyra was gone.

She wasn't off sulking. While Ava had been out scouring the farmland for Nolan, Lyra had been making her escape.

Dang if it didn't hit Ava like a punch to the gut. Like she

was still just a little girl coming home from school to find her mother's bedroom door ajar, her closet empty.

Classic Lyra. Come in, make a mess of everything, and then walk away and leave everyone else to clean it up. Deep down, she knew it was for the best. If Gran ever found out that her daughter had wanted to sell the farm out from underneath her, Ava wasn't sure she'd ever forgive her. And more than anything, Gran needed to heal in peace. But that didn't mean that seeing the bare hangers in the closet didn't make Ava's stomach ache. She just hoped that her mother would stop in San Jose on her way out and say goodbye to Gran.

The phone in her pocket buzzed, and again, for a fleeting second, she hoped it was Nolan. Instead, it was the alarm she'd set to remind her about Phoenix's meds. She shoved back a wave of disappointment and headed downstairs.

The golden retriever's tail thumped rapidly against the floor when Ava walked into the kitchen, but he stayed in his cozy bed and let her bring him the rolled-up lunchmeat. He only needed pills twice a day now. Despite eating normally and walking well, it would still be a while before it was safe for him to run and jump. The dog still spent most of his time dozing inside. Healing from a trauma like that took a lot of energy.

Ava sat on the kitchen floor, leaning back against the wall and idly stroking Phoenix's head where it rested in her lap. That's where she was when a familiar knock sounded on the kitchen door. A moment later, Nolan opened the door and poked his head inside.

"Hi," he said quietly.

"Hi," Ava returned.

Nolan walked in, closing the door behind him, and sat down on the kitchen floor.

She had been working so hard to try to keep Hoffman Farm afloat. Surely, he knew...

"I would never sell the farm." Ava's voice came out low and sad as hurt bloomed in her chest. "Not while Gran's alive. I can't even imagine selling it after she's gone, quite frankly."

Nolan nodded slowly and leaned forward to pet Phoenix, his hand inches from hers. "I know. I'm sorry."

The relief that flowed through her was short-lived.

"So why did you storm off?"

"It caught me off guard. Seeing you there with those real estate printouts, with your mother and that vulture Belinda..." Nolan shook his head, his expression closed. "I thought Lyra might have wrung an agreement out of you. Guilted you into going along with what she wanted."

"Why would you think that?"

"Because that's what she did to me," he said quietly, still looking down at Phoenix.

Ava stared at him, uncomprehending. "What do you mean?"

"She's the one who convinced me to leave. Before graduation. My dad backed her up, but it was your mother who started it."

Ava's heart threw itself against her ribcage, racing like she had just run up a hill. "I don't understand."

With visible effort, Nolan brought his ocean-colored eyes up to meet hers. "She told me that if I let you come with me, I would ruin your life. She said that you deserved to go to college, and I couldn't argue with that. My dad said we'd end up homeless and hungry, and he wouldn't bail us out. He told me to take the truck and go solo. At least if I messed up, I'd only have to worry about myself." He shook his head miserably. "I shouldn't have listened, but I did. I was young and scared and stupid. And I wanted more for you than I could give you. But I should have talked to you first. We could have figured it out together. I can't tell you how many times since then I've..." Nolan took a deep breath and paused. His eyes flicked from her eyes to her lips, then to her hair as he brushed a stray strand out of her face. "It was the worst mistake of my life, Ava. I've always regretted it."

Lyra. The ruiner of all things good. The unilateral decider of fates.

Anger swelled her chest, but before it could dig in its claws, she shoved it back.

Nope. Not this time. She had happiness within arm's reach, and she wasn't throwing it away.

Ava grabbed the front of Nolan's shirt and pulled him to her, kissing him right there on Gran's kitchen floor.

She should be angry at him too...for hiding the truth from her all these years. Furious, even. But all she felt was relief. Relief that she hadn't been crazy. That he'd cared about her as much as she had about him. That he hadn't wanted to leave her behind.

"I never stopped loving you," Nolan murmured, his face still so close to hers that the tip of his nose brushed her cheek. "Even when I tried to. Even when I was on the other side of the world. You would come to me in my dreams."

Ava took a ragged breath in, thinking of how the memory of her first love had haunted her like a ghost. And all that time...

"I was young and scared and stupid too. Or I never would have let you leave without me." She felt a flash of guilt as she thought of her children, those amazing years of their childhood in the San Diego sunshine. "But I'm not sorry. Things worked out the way they needed to. It led us to where we are right now."

"We're here now," Nolan agreed.

And he pulled her in for another kiss.

24

Ava

"But you said she would be able to leave today."

Ava was standing in the hallway outside Gran's hospital room. Frustration and fear roiled in her stomach as she faced off with one of Gran's doctors—or tried to. He wouldn't actually meet her eyes. Just kept looking between Gran's folder and the elevator doors like he had somewhere more important to be.

"These numbers aren't quite what we were hoping for yet. I can't in good conscience discharge her just yet. We'll monitor her through the weekend and circle back on Monday."

"The whole town is coming to the café to welcome her home."

The doctor did look at her now. He gave her a brief,

condescending smile. "I think your grandmother's well-being is more important than a party, don't you?"

Ava spluttered incoherently, trying to rope her thoughts and feelings into words. Gran's well-being *was* the party. Her home, her farm, her community. Homegrown strawberries and home-cooked meals. Sea air and summer sunshine. She had hit a dead end here, with these strangers under fluorescent lights. Each time Ava visited, Gran was either unsettled or exhausted. Constantly prodded and poked, no wonder her blood pressure was still a little on the high end. The only thing that she perked up for was the promise of going home.

It was time. Ava knew it in her gut.

But before she could explain that to the doctor, he was gone. Down the hall at a speed that was just short of a jog and into the elevator just as the door closed on a group of students. A frustrated growl rose in Ava's throat, and she turned toward the nurses' station.

"No luck?" Priya said with an empathetic smile.

Ava crossed to the desk and slumped against the counter, letting it hold her up. "He wouldn't even give me a real reason."

"The reason is they don't want to be liable. If you were taking her to a long-term care facility, they would have signed off already. But in the absence of that or a registered home nurse..." She shrugged.

"We have Marisol. She *is* a registered nurse. Just not here yet."

"Marisol's great," Priya said with a nod and a cagey smile. She cocked her head and then bent low, digging into a nearby filing cabinet. Once she had collected a hefty stack of papers, she handed them over. "Look, just tell them you asked me for these. They can't stop Marge from leaving. If she signs release papers, she's good to go. Marisol already has everything she needs. If her BP doesn't go down into normal range in forty-eight hours, bring her back in."

Ava flipped through the discharge papers and looked back up at Priya. "Are you sure you won't get in trouble?"

Priya rolled her eyes. "That particular doctor will forget about Marge as soon as she walks out the door. They're stretched too thin to pay much attention to people. For some of them, it's just numbers. Just promise to keep a close eye on her blood pressure."

"We will." Ava squeezed her hand. "Thank you."

"We'll miss her. She's a spitfire."

Ava reached into her purse and pulled out one of the new business cards she'd made for the café. "If you're ever in the area, we'd love to see you and treat you to a nice meal."

Priya took the card and smiled. "I'll take you up on that. I don't get over that way enough."

"We'll see you soon, then."

"Take care."

When Ava went into Gran's room, her grandmother was slumped in the hospital bed, staring out at her grim, gray view of the parking lot.

"What did he say?" she asked without looking up. She already knew the answer.

"He said no," Ava told her. Gran gave a grim grunt of acknowledgement. "And then Priya gave me these." Ava dropped the stack of forms in front of her grandmother. Gran took in the top sheet, and her eyes brightened.

"Ooooh, skippy. You're busting me out of here?"

"It's your call, Gran. The hospital won't be liable if we leave before the doctor says you're fully ready."

Her grandmother let out a snort. "I've been ready for days. And frankly, if I don't get out of here, *I'm* liable...to hurt someone. Probably that danged doctor, if you really want to know."

Ava grinned at her and shook her head. "You're too much."

"Don't just stand there grinning. Give me a pen! I can't wait to sleep in my own bed. With my own pillows. Pillows that smell like sunshine and cotton instead of bleach."

Ten minutes later, Gran was still extolling the virtues of home as Ava pushed her out the front doors of the hospital in the electric blue wheelchair she'd purchased secondhand.

Gran winced and narrowed her eyes as the morning sunlight hit her face, but her smile was dazzling.

"Ahhh...Finally," she sighed.

Summoned by a text from Ava, Nolan pulled her CRV up right in front of them. He helped Gran into the front seat, then loaded her wheelchair and climbed in back next to two of the farm dogs. Gran nearly cried with happiness as the hound dog and the pit bull lunged forward to lick her face.

"Back, beasts," Nolan rumbled, pulling them off of the center console. Ava laughed as she settled into the driver's seat and closed her door. She turned to Gran.

"Home?"

Gran smiled at her and squeezed her hand. "Home."

The ride was quiet. Gran's time in the hospital had left her pale and tired. More fragile than Ava had ever seen her. And when they finally drove through the back gate of Hoffman Farm, Nolan hopping in and out of the car to open the gate and secure it behind them, Ava was shocked to see tears streaming down her grandmother's face.

Had she *ever* seen Gran cry?

"Gran? You okay?" Ava eased one foot onto the brake pedal, slowing their downhill progress to a few miles per hour.

Maybe she'd made a mistake...

Gran nodded rapidly and brushed away her tears. "It's just so beautiful."

Ava patted Gran's knee and then returned her right hand to the steering wheel, looking out over the rolling green hills of the farm. From where they were, they couldn't see the highway. This vantage point gave the illusion of strawberry fields stretching straight out to the wide blue Pacific. One of Nolan's hands eclipsed Gran's shoulder, and she put her small, blue-veined one on top of it.

They had a few hours before the combination homecoming party and grand reopening of the Redwood Café, but already there were a dozen cars parked out front. Ava recognized Toni's battered green truck and Echo's Cadillac. A massive WELCOME HOME banner painted with sunflowers and strawberries hung above the front porch. As soon as Ava parked, her car was surrounded by well-wishers.

Nolan climbed out of the car, dogs at his heels, and retrieved Gran's wheelchair from the back. He and Marisol eased Gran into it while Lucia chattered at her and Echo draped strings of beads around her neck.

"Give an old woman some space, would you?" Gran shouted, half-laughing, her cheeks filling with color.

"Do you want to go inside and rest a while before your party?" Ava asked her.

"That is the last thing in the world I want to do right now. I'll be glad to sleep in my own bed tonight, but I have no intention of going inside before then. I want to see my garden."

Grateful that she had invested in a chair that could traverse dirt and wood chips, Ava obliged. As the others fell away and returned to party prep, Ava navigated Gran's chair around to the side of the house, where her huge garden stretched from the porch to the apple trees.

"Oh." Gran's voice caught in her throat. She sounded close to tears again. "Would you look at that."

Despite Gran's absence, the garden looked as beautiful as it ever had. Tomato plants stretched toward the sky, smelling like summer sunshine. They were all decked out in yellow flowers and little green fruits. The Thai Pink Egg tomatoes were covered in bright white ovals that would turn flamingo-pink as they ripened. Marigolds bloomed all around them, covering the ground in golden fireworks. Further on, herbs and zinnias filled the rows with rainbow blossoms.

"Greta's been working in the garden every day," Ava said quietly, leaning close to Gran's ear. "She planted all the seeds you ordered last year and followed your garden plan as best as she could. And Toni came by last week to fill any bare spots with starts and transplants."

"You girls." Gran's voice was thick with tears. She shook her head and patted Ava's hand where it rested on her shoulder. "How did I get so lucky?"

"You reap what you sow," Ava told her. She spotted Greta among the sunflowers and waved her over with a smile.

"I'm going to go make sure everything's on track with the café, all right? I'll send Marisol over."

"No need to fuss," Gran told her, eyes still riveted on her garden. Ava kissed her cheek and walked away without arguing. The truth was, Gran was helpless. She was too weak to move her wheelchair on her own, utterly dependent on the people around her for everything. Luckily, there were enough of them. Still, Ava knew how important Gran's independence was to her. She had tried to find an electric wheelchair before Gran came home, but there was nothing in their budget that would be able to get around the farm. Gran would just have to let them help her until she was on her feet again. She was scheduled to be fitted with a prosthetic foot next month.

Ava trotted over to the café and through the back door. The kitchen was busy with new hires, the air thick with the smell of strawberry tarts and tomato soup. In the front room, Toni was setting out bouquets on each of the fresh-painted tables.

"Ava!" Toni set her flowers aside and pulled her down for a kiss on the cheek. "Where's Gran?"

"She's in the garden."

"Sweet." Toni pulled Ava over to another table to show her the flower crown she had made. It was glorious, three inches tall and comprised of a fiery riot of different varieties of calendula. "Marisol's going to help her into the new dress Echo bought her, and then I'm going to crown her homecoming queen."

Ava chuckled. "Good luck getting her out of the garden."

"Marisol can do it. That woman is a force of nature."

"You're probably right."

Toni carefully picked up the flower crown and asked, "Have you seen Maggie yet?"

Ava's heart lurched in her chest. "Maggie's here?"

"Yeah, she's–" Toni cut herself off with a laugh, because Ava was already sprinting out the front door. And there was her daughter, draping borrowed tablecloths over plastic picnic tables. Her thick dark hair was piled on top of her head, and she looked breathtakingly beautiful in a flowy floral sundress. Ava nearly tackled her with a hug, and Maggie cackled with surprise.

"Mom! When did you get back? Where's Gran?"

"I'll tell you in two minutes. Just let me look at you." Ava reached up and took Maggie's face in her hands. The dark hair and long, straight nose were just like her father's, but Maggie's bright blue eyes were pure Hoffman.

"You are so weird," Maggie complained through slightly squashed lips, but she made no move to escape. Instead, she stepped in for a second hug.

Ava paid no attention as an unfamiliar car crunched over the gravel and parked nearby, but she jumped to attention at the sound of her son's voice.

"Hey, Mags!" Ryan hopped out of the car and trotted across the yard. His mom and sister met him halfway in a high-speed collision that turned into a laughing hug. "Hey, Mom. We made it."

"No thanks to this guy," Eli muttered from a few feet away. "He made me take the One the whole way."

"I'll take waves over cows, thanks," Ryan said. Ava stepped back and looked at her handsome son, who was a full head taller than her. With almost-black hair and dark hazel eyes, he looked just like his dad. His hair was as long as it had ever been, hanging in waves past his chin and highlighted by his time in the sun, and Ava's chest ached at the thought of his coming buzz cut. But she was still smiling as she tucked a stray strand behind his ear.

"I'm so glad you could make it."

"Wouldn't miss it. Where's Gran?"

"She'll be out in a bit," Toni said, appearing behind Ava's shoulder. "She's inside getting all dolled up."

"Aunt Toni!" Ryan caught her up in a hug that lifted her feet from the ground. "When did you get so little?"

Toni laughed and gave her godson a playful shove. "Shut up."

"So." Ryan turned back to his mom. "How can we help?"

The whole town turned up in support of Gran, and hundreds of tourists passed through to sample the offerings of the new Redwood Café. Ava let her capable employees handle the tourist traffic while she stayed close to Gran, relaxing in the shade of tents that farmers market vendors had loaned them for the day. Echo flitted through the crowd, bright as a hummingbird in her emerald silk. Yolanda was there, along with a new hire that presented Gran with a handmade shawl adorned with a sunflower pattern. The whole Flores clan showed up, and Ava was floored when Toni's stepmother presented her with a check for twenty thousand dollars.

"I don't understand," she stammered, holding the piece of paper gingerly in her hands.

"It's from all of us," Patricia explained. "You didn't see the fundraiser I posted on Facebook?"

Ava shook her head, mute.

"Marge means a lot to all of us. We wanted to cover the

cost of an electric wheelchair, plus as much of the rehab process as we could. I know it will be a long road, but we all want to see her back on her feet. Well, foot."

Ava nodded, feeling vaguely guilty for the years that she and Toni had spent referring to Patricia as the Wicked Witch of the Woods. By the time she found her voice again, Patricia was already gone, mingling with friends by the potato salad.

Out in the yard, Juniper was spinning Lucia in circles. The moment she stopped, her little cousins ran up to beg for a turn. Gran was watching them, enjoying a moment of quiet, and Ava went to sit next to her before the crowd converged again.

"Hey, Gran?"

"What's up, buttercup?" Gran reached over to take Ava's hand in hers, still watching Juniper and Maggie play with a crowd of small children.

"I want to stay."

"Aw, Ava. I love you." Gran squeezed her hand. "And I'm grateful for your help, but I can't let you do that. We'll be all right. It's time for you to get your life back."

"No. I *want* to stay."

Gran turned to look at her, sky-blue eyes wide. "You mean...move here for good?"

"With Ryan going, and the café, and you–" Ava's explanation was cut off when Gran pulled her in for a hug with a sudden burst of strength that was as encouraging as it was surprising. "Is that okay?"

"My home is your home, Avalon. Nothing would make me happier."

"Lyra...I mean Mom...she's, um–"

"She's gone?" Gran interrupted as she pulled away.

Ava nodded. "I'm so sorry."

Gran's brow furrowed for a moment before smoothing. "You aren't her keeper, kiddo. She marches to the beat of her own drum. And that beat will bring her back home again eventually." She gave Ava's hand a squeeze. "I've made peace with that. I hope someday you can too. Now, let's enjoy this amazing, momentous occasion, shall we?"

Ava nodded, her throat too tight to speak. Her grandmother was so forgiving and so wise. She wasn't sure she'd even get to the point of making peace with the person that Lyra was, but the proof that it was possible gave her hope. And sometimes, hope was all a person needed.

Gran was asleep in bed before sunset with Phoenix curled up a few feet away and Marisol studying in the living room until Ava went home for the night. Ava was trying to help clean up the many tents and tables that had been borrowed for the party, but their owners kept brushing her off with friendly smiles in favor of doing it themselves. Finally, she gave up and went to find Nolan, who was luring the chickens into their coop with a handful of grain. His face lit up when he saw her.

"A successful homecoming," Nolan said as he locked the chickens in for the night.

"And a successful grand opening."

"No small feat."

Ava nodded and leaned into him, suddenly bone tired. Nolan brought his arms around her and moved one hand up and down her back, massaging the tense muscles on either side of her spine. Slowly, the tension Ava carried drained away. She still hadn't told Nolan her plans for the future yet. She'd wanted to talk to her grandmother first, but now seemed like the perfect time.

"I told Gran that I want to move home."

Nolan's hand stopped moving, and Ava leaned back to look at him.

"You're staying?" he asked, his expression guarded. "For good?"

Ava nodded slowly, lost in the dark teal of his eyes, the thump of his heart. She felt a sudden jolt of fear. What if *he* didn't want to stay? Nolan had been all around the world. How long would he be content with running a tiny California farm?

"Are you?" she asked. "Staying?"

He grinned then and pressed a firm kiss to her lips.

"If you're here? I'm not going anywhere."

25

Toni

Toni was still buzzing with contentment when she got home from the grand opening that night. Gran was back home where she belonged, and Ava was here to stay. Juniper was at Lizzie's house tonight, babysitting the girls so that Lizzie could pick up an extra shift. That meant that Toni had a quiet evening to herself followed by a whole summer with a niece who was eager to help with garden chores and farmers markets.

Life was pretty perfect.

She grabbed a neglected stack of mail from inside and sat down on her porch to enjoy the night air. Aside from envelopes containing seed packets, Toni's mail tended to languish for a while before she opened it. It was mostly junk, anyhow. She flipped through it slowly, tossing nearly all of it into a pile bound for the recycling bin.

A letter from her landlords. That was odd. They had moved down to San Diego years ago, and she never heard from them. Toni ripped the envelope open and unfolded the papers.

Antonia Flores,

PLEASE TAKE NOTICE that your tenancy of the premises is terminated effective at the end of a sixty (60) day period after service on you of this notice.

It was a damned form-letter lease termination.

Under *Reason for Termination* and a checked box next to *No-fault Just Cause,* her landlady had scrawled, *I'm so sorry, Toni! My husband is set on selling, and I just couldn't hold him off anymore. I know you'll land on your feet! Thanks for taking such good care of our property! You'll see below that we've waived your rent for July. Best of luck!*

Toni read the whole thing through several times before it really sank in. She had less than two months to find a new place to live. Just a few weeks to relocate her market garden.

In California.

In the summertime.

Not good...

Did you enjoy meeting the folks of Redwood Grove? Check out Toni's story in Redwood Meadow, coming summer of 2023!

And stay tuned for a new series from Shayla Cherry, coming later this year, starting with **Big Island Sunrise**...

. . .

Dive into an uplifting saga of found family, sisterhood, and new beginnings.

Emma Kealoha is still reeling from the death of her husband, but it's her son's pain that cuts deepest of all. Six-year-old Kai has been spiraling out of control since losing his dad, and Emma doesn't know how to help him. When Kai inherits his grandfather's property in Hawaii, Emma catches a glimpse of light through the fog of their grief. Flying to the Big Island to manage Kai's inheritance is the perfect opportunity to escape the suffocating sympathy of Redwood Grove. Maybe Hawaii's green mountains and black sand beaches will breathe some new life into her tired soul.

Lani King left her abusive husband -- for good this time. She and her daughter move home to the Big Island, but Lani can't seem to get her feet on solid ground. Staying with Emma could give Lani a chance to catch her breath while she figures out what's next. A new romance is peeking over the horizon, but how can she open up to love when her ex won't even sign the divorce papers?

With some help from their extended family, Emma and Lani work to make the old Kealoha place livable again. As the wild land and aloha spirit begin to mend Kai's broken heart, Emma wonders if she can build a life for them there. It won't be easy. Between tropical storms and Lani's vindictive ex, this fresh start will be hard won... if they can make it happen at all.